GIDEON'S MEN

Mr. Marric weaves a continuous exciting narrative which gives the impression of perfect authenticity; yet this is, in fact, the product of . . . a veteran writer whose art is so skilful as almost to conceal itself.

*Books by J. J. Marric in the
Ulverscroft Large Print Series:*

GIDEON'S DAY
GIDEON'S WEEK
GIDEON'S RISK
GIDEON'S LOT
GIDEON'S POWER
GIDEON'S RIVER
GIDEON'S RIDE
GIDEON'S FIRE
GIDEON'S MONTH
GIDEON'S MEN

◆

This Large Print Edition
is published by kind permission of
HODDER & STOUGHTON LTD
London

J. J. MARRIC

GIDEON'S MEN

Complete and Unabridged

ULVERSCROFT
Leicester

First printed in 1972

First Large Print Edition
published April 1975
SBN 85456 325 3

This special large print edition is
made and printed in England for
F. A. Thorpe, Glenfield, Leicestershire

CONTENTS

Chapter		page
1	Great Occasion	1
2	Morning	16
3	First Capture — First Crime	31
4	Morning Reports	46
5	Collapse	60
6	Rescue Effort	75
7	Mob	92
8	No Pause . . .	105
9	Medley	122
10	Murderer	140
11	Despair and Joy	154
12	The Bicycle	171
13	Stand-by	194
14	Briefing	209
15	The Rent Collector	221
16	Short Term	239
17	Search in London	256
18	Search on Dartmoor	273
19	The Witnesses	290
20	Visitors	306
21	Long and Short Term	320

CHAPTER I

GREAT OCCASION

"GOOD evening, Commander . . . Mrs. Gideon, nice to see you again."

"Hallo, Geo— Commander! . . . Hallo, Kate, you look glorious."

"Commander, a long time since we met . . . May I present my wife . . . Good evening, Mrs. Gideon, this is a truly great occasion . . . Darling, I don't think you've met Mrs. Gideon, the Commander's wife."

"Hiya, George! . . . Hallo, Kate."

"Good evening, sir . . . Mrs. Gideon . . . My wife . . ."

The line of people approaching the reception party at this 50th Criminal Investigation Department Ball seemed never-ending. The men wore tails, with here and there a black tie and dinner jacket, and all the women were dressed for a great occasion, most of the dresses long, many of them new, a good sprinkling of white with here and there a black setting off the rainbow colours of the rest.

Gideon, massive in tails a shade too tight, hardly surprising since they were twenty-five years old, was very content. Kate, next to him, in a black dress brightened with designs embroidered in a dozen colours and holding a bouquet of spring flowers, was a woman to be proud of. And the occasion put life into her blue grey eyes, predominantly grey in this artificial light. She glowed. Now and again a woman as tall and nearly as striking came up with her husband, their names echoing from the stentorian voice of the Mayor's toast-master, who stood at the door, back to a huge bank of flowers in which a motif had been cleverly designed reading

C.I.D.

in a variety of colours, with the badge of London's Metropolitan Police on either side. The line of people stretched along a wide passage which led from the front of the Melham Town Hall to this ballroom, which was as flamboyantly Victorian as could be, with huge chandeliers and mirrors round the walls above the red plush seats and the brightly gilded framework of the seats and chairs set about round tables where eight could sit in comfort and ten or even twelve if all sat elbow to elbow.

The reception had been going on for nearly half an hour.

Here came Tom Riddell, Chief Detective Superintendent, a brown-eyed, brown-haired man, once very massive, somehow a big business-looking man frequently over-confident and aggressive but beginning to show his age. His little, grey-haired wife was like a gaily-decked sparrow with dyed feathers.

"Hallo, Tom . . . Good evening, Mrs. Riddell . . ."

And here was Matt Honiwell, a big, cuddly man with brown curly hair hardly showing grey, several years older than Riddell although he looked so much the younger. With Honiwell was a woman Gideon hadn't seen before: tall, severe-looking, striking. Who? Gideon wondered. Honiwell had lost his wife some years ago and appeared to have settled down to a bachelor existence. His handclasp, as always, was firm and quick.

"Congratulations, Commander . . ." He had a gentle voice, and spoke as if each

3

word was considered. "May I present Mrs. Jameson — Netta Jameson?"

Netta Jameson had a pleasant, controlled voice; she was a woman of noticeable poise.

"Good evening, Commander Gideon."

They shook hands; hers was colder than Honiwell's, but her grip was as quick and firm.

Gideon turned to Kate, as Mrs. Riddell moved on.

"You know Matt Honiwell, of course . . . But I don't think you know Mrs. Jameson."

If there was a woman here who matched Kate in appearance, it was Honiwell's guest. Nearly as tall, with a full figure yet surprisingly slender waist, she wore a white gown with gold embroidery, simple yet very elegant. And her smile warmed when she saw Kate, as if recognising that she had met a kindred spirit. Kate warmed, too.

But the line moved on, remorselessly.

This was *the* Criminal Investigation Department's Ball, and though Gideon knew most of the guests, he became more and more surprised at how many he did know. Hundreds: *thousands*? Man after man, woman after woman, first the Commissioner, Sir Reginald Scott-Marle and his wife; the distinguished, elegant words seemed to fit them like their attire; next to Scott-Marle were the Commissioner of the City Police and the Lord Mayor of London and his lady, resplendent in their historic finery. Next came the Assistant Commissioner for Crime, a man named Donaldson and one of the few men Gideon disliked; Donaldson, a bachelor, had his sister with him; they both had the stamp of the military about them, belonged more to the Army than to the police. Next was the Commander of the Women Police, a compact, attractive-looking woman with her husband whose silver hair made him look very much older than his wife.

Finally came Gideon and Kate, the last in the line of the reception party, only just inside the ballroom. This was seething with people, among whom was Gideon's Deputy Commander, Alec Hobbs, with Penelope, Gideon's youngest daughter, both there to guide the guests to vacant tables, to help organise the function although most of the organising had been finished long in advance. Penelope radiated youth and young womanhood; at twenty-five, she had become a permanent member of the B.B.C. Symphony Orchestra, playing the piano, especially solos, with high competence which might develop into brilliance. Nearly twenty years older than Penelope, Alec Hobbs had made no secret of his love for her. In his immaculate tails, possessing an extra "something" it was hard to define, he looked almost right for her; it was as if they had already grown into complementing each other.

Gideon had little chance to speculate about them, but he did begin to worry a little about Kate. The Assistant Commissioner met an old friend and held up the line while he chatted — that was somehow characteristic of the man, who was seldom considerate of others. But this gave Gideon a chance to say to Kate:

"Tired, love?"

"I *have* been fresher!" But Kate's eyes still glowed.

"You can go and rest, you know. Penny would love to stand in for you."

"*Could* she?"

"Of course." The fact that Kate was even prepared to consider this proved how tired she must be feeling. She had been ill with a fatigued heart, a few months ago, and still needed to be careful and not to over-exert herself. Gideon caught Hobbs's eye quickly, for Hobbs had "fly" eyes which enabled him to see around a wide perimeter. He looked young and his features, regular but often emotionally dull, held an expression of excitement and pleasure, stimulated by Penelope at least as much as the occasion. Gideon remembered him at this very function, several years ago, when his now dead wife had already been showing signs of the disease — leukaemia — which had eventually killed her. At that time Hobbs had looked ten years older than he did now.

The private lives of the men had a vital bearing on their work in the Force; this was a fact which Gideon realised more and more as the years passed.

"Yes, George?" Hobbs inquired from his side.

"Could you find Kate a good spot to sit — not the V.I.P.s' table, yet — and ask Penny to stand in for her?"

"Now Penny *will* be the belle of the Ball," Hobbs rejoiced. "I'll fetch her. The Honiwells are with the Riddells — will their table do?"

"Just right." Trust Hobbs!

In a moment Penny was standing at Gideon's side, and in some almost uncanny way, she became more mature, suiting the occasion in both mood and manner. She also glowed. As a teenager she had been a tomboy and rather *gamine* in appearance, now her snub nose had become *retroussé* and her nice lips quite beautiful; there wasn't a better complexion in the ballroom.

"Mummy's not ill, is she?" she asked.

"She just needs to get off her feet . . . Hallo, Hugh!" The Chief Detective Superintendent who now came up was Hugh Rollo, one of the Yard's glamour boys with a well-deserved reputation as a ladies' man. There was something in the expression on his pleasant face which made his reputation easy to understand, not so much a "come hither" look as one of natural boldness. With him, to Gideon's astonishment, was one of the senior members of the typing-pool at the Yard, Sabrina Sale, a woman in her early fifties, gentle-looking, nicely dressed in powder-blue trimmed with silver. Surely she and Rollo —

"Good evening, Commander." Sabrina's grey eyes smiled, she looked younger than he recalled from her many visits to his office to take down letters. "I hope this will be a most memorable evening for you."

"In every way," Gideon said.

"How very *gallant*!" Sabrina's hand lingered in his perhaps a moment longer than was strictly necessary. Rollo was talking gaily with Penelope, whom he obviously fascinated. Gideon did not want to have to tell him to move on, but this was beginning to hold up the line. Then Hobbs appeared and touched Rollo's arm lightly; Rollo took the hint and crooked his arm for Sabrina. As they went off he saw that she was one of the few wearing a short dress, and noticed not for the first time what very nice legs she had.

Fifty or sixty more couples filed past, until even Gideon began to feel the strain. Then his lips widened at the sight of a slim, Jamaican woman with a scarred lip which did little to detract from her honey-coloured, broad-featured beauty. A few months ago she had helped to trap the ringleaders of an anti-apartheid group who planned to go far beyond peaceful demonstrations; one of them had slashed her lips and she had been lucky not to be disfigured far worse than this; lucky indeed to be alive. She wore a silver lamé dress, very simply cut, and her hair style, of plentiful loose curls, suited her.

She had a beautiful name: Juanita Concepcion. With her was Charles Henry of Hampstead Division, the man under whose orders she had been at the time of her injuries. During the case, Gideon had sensed that there was more in the relationship than that of a Divisional superintendent and a member of the Force.

Did this prove it?

Henry was a man of medium height, with gingery fair hair and pleasant but broad features.

"Commander."

"Charles, how are you? . . . Good to see you again, Miss Concepcion . . . My daughter Penelope."

"Yes, we've met," said Henry.

Gideon felt the gaze from honey-brown eyes and remembered this girl saying only a short time before she had been attacked: "You just have to believe in something, sir, and I believe in law and order." That had been at a time when racialism had already been savage and ugly in parts of London. She was quite short, the top of her head coming only just above his shoulder. The wound had healed so that it gave her a hint of a smile even when in repose and revealed the gold-cap of a tooth in her lower jaw.

"You're very kind to remember me, Commander." Her voice was gentle and yet noticeably resonant.

"You aren't easy to forget," he retorted. "For what you are and for what you've done."

Her eyes glowed with pleasure, and she turned to Penny, while Gideon saw more crowding at the door. Now he had held the line up! He was a fine one to blame Donaldson! The toast-master began to call the names again and the flow started afresh.

* * *

At last, the reception was over.

Now Gideon sat with Kate and Scott-Marle, a tall, spare, aloof-looking man, too thin, his cheeks almost hollow. He was with his young wife who couldn't be much more than thirty-five: his second wife, vivacious, looking about her as she sat, but she didn't sit for long, she loved to dance. Donaldson and his grey-haired sister were formal dancers and they sat at the table more than any of the others. Gideon and Kate danced the opening waltz, and then — by a consent built up over the years — danced with others, mostly old friends but some quite new. Superintendents' wives, who were eager to call him George, Chief Inspectors' wives who lingered over "Commander", mostly middle-aged whom he had known for many years.

This whole ballroom was filled with people who were part of his life.

They came from every one of London's twenty-four Divisions; from Mayfair and from Bethnal Green, from lofty, arty Hampstead and from lowly, arty Fulham. They came from the Thames Division and, as guests, from the City of London Police and from the Port of London Authority Police; from the outer suburbs where crime was thin to Soho, where it was the stock-in-trade of so many who lived and worked there. Every part of London, then, with men and women of every rank; from the Home Office, who controlled the Yard to the pathological staff. Nearly everyone who was to do with the job of trying to prevent crime in London and in catching criminals was here: in all, over twelve hundred people.

And he, Gideon, was the man in charge of them all in their daily work.

It was a good, gratifying feeling.

Some who would have liked to be present were on duty, of course, but it was easy to forget the absent faces. Easy, amid this mass of crime-fighters, to forget crime: to forget that crimes were being carried out all over London at this very moment; to forget that murders were being committed, or at least violent assaults; banks were being burgled, shops robbed, cars stolen, pockets picked, handbags snatched, confidence tricksters busy with their spiel, young girls lying beneath men who had attacked them out of the darkness, some virgins, knowing what it was like to be brutally possessed for the first time. Deflowered. Every kind of crime in London's streets, then . . . and here two orchestras playing and the lights so bright and the dancing so gay, while in a room on the floor above, huge tables groaned under food prepared by a hundred pairs of hands for a host of ravenous men. Over on one side of this room was the huge bar, crowded with men out-numbering the women by at least two to one.

Rollo came up to ask Kate to dance, and Gideon went across to Sabrina Sale. She danced a waltz like a feather, and somehow rested in his arms as if this were where she belonged. She looked up at him all the time, with her almost teasing smile. He was content to dance and not talk, never quite sure what he felt about this woman, never quite sure that he ought to feel what he did.

"You dance beautifully," he observed.

"You dance as I hoped you would," she retorted. "Commandingly."

"And Rollo?"

Her eyes were very bright.

"He dances as if he can't get you off the floor soon enough, Commander. You can imagine the rest."

"I don't think I'd better. Do you often come to functions as his partner?"

"Yes," she answered. "He needs a chaperone, as it were, and I love dancing and know enough people here to be sure of being able to dance with someone." She seemed to nestle against his chest and arm. "Your wife is the most strikingly beautiful woman here."

"Yes," said Gideon, simply, and his eyes teased. "Do you think Rollo is dancing with her as if he cannot get her off the floor quickly enough?"

Sabrina didn't answer at once; and then, as the orchestra swung into the last beats of the tune, she looked at him very directly, with no hint of a smile in her eyes, and answered:

"The one thing I have discovered is that no person knows what any other is thinking. Husband and wife, mother and child, father and son, big boss and worker — even Sabrina Sale and the Commander."

The music stopped.

"Thank you," she said, "that was quite beautiful."

The odd thing was that he thought she really meant that; he was sure she had enjoyed their dancing with some special savour.

And so had he.

CHAPTER 2

MORNING

"WELL," Gideon asked Kate, "wasn't that the best of them all?"

"I really think it was," she agreed.

"And Penny seemed to be in a seventh heaven."

"So did Alec," Kate replied thoughtfully. "I wonder how things will work out between them."

Gideon didn't speak at once.

They were in the back of a Yard car, being driven to their home in Fulham. Alec and Penny had gone off, perhaps to a night club, perhaps to join a group from the Ball. It had finished at one o'clock, with "Auld Lang Syne" and "God Save the Queen", the Gideons, the Scott-Marles, the Donaldsons and the Mayor in the middle of great circles of people holding hands and swaying to and fro to the strains of "Auld Lang Syne". The official party had broken up quickly, the hall had emptied smoothly and now tired-eyed cleaners and waiters were beginning the task of clearing up.

Where had Sabrina Sale gone? Off with Hugh Rollo? Was her association with him as innocent as she had made it seem? Innocent? What was the matter with him to ask such a word of a woman of her maturity and a man whom half of Scotland Yard called "Don Juan"? He shrugged the thought away.

Kate's hand was in his, cool but limp; she must be very tired indeed, and he hoped she hadn't overdone it. Scott-Marle had danced with her in the Gay Gordons and they had appeared to love it with breathless abandon. Honiwell had danced with her several times. Honiwell with his tall eagle of a woman and Riddell with his little sparrow. Riddell, once almost a competitor with Rollo, had danced very little. He was a harassed, worried man and Gideon could now understand that he was unlikely to get help from his wife.

He, Gideon, knew much of what was on Riddell's mind; and much that was on Honiwell's, too.

Two investigation problems were building up at the Yard; two which could not be more different in nature or in range, and Riddell and Honiwell were involved in addition to many others.

Riddell had begun to investigate a number of crimes arising out of Britain's new social problem — race and colour. Honiwell had started to work on an investigation into a case once thought to be over and done with, the murder of a woman in a London suburb, a murder for which the wrong man might have been found guilty.

In the first place, these were problems within problems, and if a thing was wrong in a community, it was always likely to become police business sooner or later. Overcrowding in houses, for instance, led to frayed tempers, anger, fights, often to murder or manslaughter; discrimination in a factory could lead to conflict between groups, strikes, picketing, and so to crimes or at least crowd control. Very little which happened in London was certain to remain outside the orbit of the police.

These two cases were very much within that orbit, the first especially so.

In several parts of London, overcrowding was so rife among Jamaican, Indian and

Pakistani immigrants-now-residents that crimes arising from these conditions were far too frequent. And there were indications that certain groups of white fanatics were aggravating the difficulties of integration in every way they could. Riddell had been assigned to this months ago, and had proved at first to be pathologically prejudiced against non-whites. The prejudice had never shown itself before this investigation, as far as Gideon knew, but when assigning a man to such a delicate investigation he should have made quite sure. So, to some degree, anything that went wrong would be Gideon's fault.

Of course if he carried that argument to a logical conclusion, then all investigating failures were due to his seconding the wrong man, and this was nonsense. On the other hand he should have taken extra care where this problem was concerned. To complicate and in one way to make it worse, Riddell had found a Pakistani girl dead of neglect and starvation in a hole beneath the staircase of a rotting house in an overcrowded district of Notting Hill. It had given him a severe attack of conscience. He had been on holiday for several weeks since then and was only just back on duty. When they had last met, he had wanted Gideon to take him off the investigation. Would he still want that?

Honiwell, already deeply involved in the other case, had been standing in for Riddell; Gideon had to see him in the morning. Or rather, *this* morning! It was already two o'clock.

They turned into Harrington Street and the driver pulled up smoothly outside one of the tall, terraced buildings of red brick, with white-painted eaves and woodwork showing clearly in the light of street lamps. The light was good enough to show the neat patch of grass, the neatly trimmed box-hedge. The driver jumped out and opened the car door for Kate, and Gideon got out on the offside and joined her.

"Good-night, Castle."

"Good-night, sir."

"Were you at the Ball?"

"*And* my wife, sir. She had a wonderful time." Castle, who often drove Gideon, seldom made any comment. "If you don't mind me saying so, sir, these functions have been much better since you became Commander."

"Really?" remarked Gideon, startled.

"Why?" asked Kate, mischief in her eyes.

"Well, Mrs. Gideon, there's a kind of family atmosphere, the Commander's a kind of — er — a kind of father-figure. I hope I'm not speaking out of place?"

"Perfectly all right," Gideon replied gruffly. "Flattering, in fact. I'm glad your wife enjoyed it. Good-night again."

"Good-night, sir."

The quiet purr of the car's engine was still sounding when Gideon closed the hall door, while Kate put on the passage and the landing light. Penelope had a key, so he could close but not bolt the door. Kate was at the foot of the stairs.

"How does it feel like to be a father-figure, darling?"

"Oh, nonsense," he retorted.

"There's no nonsense about it," Kate said. "It's exactly what you are to the C.I.D.! Love, do you mind if I go straight up?"

"Of course not. Like some tea? Or Ovaltine? Or anything?"

"Just a *little* warm milk would be lovely."

When he went upstairs, the milk on a tray, and a glass of cold milk for himself, Kate was ready for sleep, wearing a loose-fitting flannelette nightdress, her hair, freshly done for the Ball, now in a hairnet which somehow proved becoming. She sat up on the pillows on their big, old-fashioned double bed, while he undressed, sipping the cold milk in between movements. He looked enormous when wearing only pyjama trousers; barrel-chested, a little too heavy about the stomach but not truly fat, with less hair on his torso than might have been expected.

"What did you think of Honiwell's girl friend?" asked Gideon.

"Striking," answered Kate, "and lively and intelligent."

"Think they'll marry?" asked Gideon.

"I can tell you that for the time being, they can't," confided Kate. "Her husband won't give her a divorce although they've been separated for ten years."

"Are they anticipating the marriage bonds?" asked Gideon.

"Would it matter if they were?"

Gideon pursed his lips.

"No," he pronounced, but with an edge of doubt in his voice. "Unless it wore him down and became an obsession so that he couldn't concentrate on his work properly. No need to anticipate trouble, though." Gideon drank down the rest of his milk. "How was Hugh Rollo?"

"The perfect gentleman!"

"Trust Rollo," Gideon remarked rather drily.

He was busy with thoughts in preparation for the morning when he got into bed. Honiwell, Riddell and Rollo. Honiwell was too involved in the old case to be able to concentrate on the racial one, and Rollo might be exactly the man to take over from him, with two or three other superintendents; one of them would have to be in charge but others would be needed, and at least six Divisions were deeply concerned. It was a major operation.

"Deep thoughts?" asked Kate.

"Very. About tomorrow's briefing."

"George," said Kate, snuggling her back against him. He was pleasantly aware of her body, her warmth, her familiarity.

"Yes, dear?"

"Do you know Sabrina Sale well?"

23

He was startled into sudden stillness, almost a tension through his whole body, and one Kate would be instantly aware of. He thought for a moment that Kate might have been very conscious of his dancing with Sabrina, then rejected it as unlikely: so he relaxed.

"Fairly well," he answered. "She's my favourite stenographer from the shorthand typing pool. Why?"

"It's none of my business, I know," said Kate, "but she wouldn't be right for Hugh Rollo, would she? And he wouldn't be right for her, would he?"

Gideon went still again, then gave a deep chuckle, partly due to relief.

"I don't know," he said. "They might get along very well, she tolerant of his peccadilloes and he glad of warm slippers and a good meal when he gets home. Did you see much of her?"

"Not much," Kate answered, and yawned. "She's a very attractive woman in her way, with a beautiful figure. If it wasn't obvious from her face that she's in her fifties I would put her down for her mid-thirties. I hope she doesn't throw herself away on Hugh."

"I could put him on night duty," Gideon remarked.

It was Kate's turn to chuckle.

In the few minutes between settling down and dropping off to sleep, Gideon considered the problem of someone to take over from Riddell, but gave more thought to the domestic aspect of the divers Yard men which had been thrown into prominence tonight. It was surprising how many of them had been widowed or divorced; how many changes of wives there had been over ten years. And if far more couples had stayed together than had parted, some of those still married obviously lived a pretty difficult home life. Riddell, for instance, and his little bird-like wife. One thing that functions like tonight's Ball achieved was a broadening of one's attitude; a deeper realisation of the casualty rate among marriages, showing presumably that the work of a policeman put more stresses on marriage than most jobs.

Or was that just his imagination?

It would be interesting to get some figures...

Quite suddenly, he fell asleep.

Nearly a hundred and fifty miles away, in Dartmoor Prison, a man named Entwhistle lay on his narrow bed in his narrow cell, thinking, going over the facts of his life time and time again, until it seemed as if he would drive himself mad. The main burden of his thoughts was that he was here, serving a life sentence after being convicted of the murder of his wife; but he had not killed her. He was shut up here, the very life being drained out of him, while his children were with relatives and the actual murderer was living somewhere, scot-free.

God! How he hated the truth!

A year ago, a prison chaplain had raised some hopes that the investigation would be reopened, but now the padre had gone overseas and it was months since Entwhistle had had the faintest grounds for hope.

He tossed and turned, tossed and turned, until at last he drifted off to sleep.

★ ★ ★

In London, much closer to Gideon, another man slept very soundly, as if his conscience were as clear as any man's.

His name was Eric Greenwood and he was the murderer of Entwhistle's wife. That had been over three years ago. He had almost forgotten it, only occasionally did he even remember that another man was in prison for the crime he had committed. He did not dream, sleeping or waking that the police were going over all the evidence in the case and that Honiwell was following a clue which had not been unearthed during the trial: Margaret Entwhistle had had a lover while her husband had been overseas on a big bridge-building contract.

* * *

Honiwell, whose mind was as sharp as his appearance was cuddly, lay thinking about two things: the investigation he was making into the Entwhistle case, and his own relationship with Netta Jameson.

They *were* lovers.

It wasn't, as in the case of Entwhistle's wife, because her husband was out of the country and she had been desperately lonely. It was simply because she had not been able to go on living with her husband, and had been legally separated for ten years — five longer than he, Honiwell, had been widowed. Her husband was an alcoholic but in his sober periods a very moralistic, puritan man. He was, moreover, under-sexed, and in their marriage sex had played very little part. He, Honiwell, could remember vividly after one of their furious, passionate embraces, when it had seemed as if they would exhaust themselves, that Netta had lain gasping in his arms, and yet managed to say:

"I thought I was frigid. Oh, Matt! I really did."

He had soothed her, touching her soft skin with his lips, fondling her body.

"Well, that's a mistake you'll never make again."

Frigid! My God!

Now, she was asleep in the bed next to him, at her flat, not his. He still had his home, and his married daughter and her husband shared it, so he could not take Netta there overnight. Well, not very easily, not without creating an anomalous situation with the family. So he spent as much time as he could here, consoling himself that it was probably as well, it was never wise for a member of the C.I.D. to allow himself to reveal that he was involved in an irregular relationship. No one would mind, officially, but if anything went wrong with a case, the Entwhistle case, for instance, this relationship might be blamed; it might conceivably be regarded as the cause of lack of concentration.

The worry on Honiwell's mind was: should he tell Gideon?

If Gideon knew then there would be a load off his own conscience; but there might be an added one on Gideon's. There really wasn't any reason to believe he would do his job any worse; in fact his own heightened emotional awareness might make him do it better.

Well, he would see how he felt in the morning. Meanwhile, one thing gave him unexpected pleasure; Kate Gideon had obviously taken to Netta, and Netta to her. At the same time, that could become a cause for anxiety: would Kate Gideon have been so warmly disposed had she known the true nature of their relationship? That was the rub. They might live in a permissive society, but my God, when they broke the outmoded conventions, what a mess it could be.

Only a mile away from Netta Jameson's flat, in a tiny apartment in Victoria, not far from the B.O.A.C. terminal in Buckingham Palace Road, Sabrina Sale lay sleeping. Alone.

CHAPTER 3

FIRST CAPTURE — FIRST CRIME

IT was a night for crime.

No policeman ever knew why but every week or two there seemed to be an aura, a kind of moon-madness, which set old lags out on the rampage, which doomed hitherto non-criminals to a life of crime and, often it seemed coincidentally, which made ordinary people commit crimes. Lovers, for instance, embittered by their loves; husbands and wives, hating their spouses; men — mostly men — driven to the wall by debt, tempted to steal from employer or from friend. And there were the parents, goaded out of their minds by crying, fretting babies, who struck the hapless victims time and time again, battering them, sometimes to death.

There was no end to the variety of crime in London; no list could be complete.

Early that night, during the hours when the Police Ball, glittering and bespangled, reached its high crescendo, the old lags were about. It was not, of course, entirely unexpected, for the man who was kind of step-brother to the policeman, the habitual criminal, knew that many top policemen were at the Ball. Whenever this was so, there was a change in atmosphere among the police of London, as if the festivities stretched out and touched every man in uniform or in plainclothes. Perhaps there was an added factor, a certain relaxation of discipline seldom evident in any particular case, but common everywhere. Whatever the cause, the old pros chanced their arm more, often quite impudent in their crimes, and many reached home to boast to sleepy wives and to demand a wifely reward.

There were, of course, those new criminals. That night several committed crimes for the first time in their lives. And there were, of course, the new policemen. One of these was P.C. Oswald, of the Ealing Division, never before out on his own. He had been through two years' training, had spent several weeks out on the beat with another, experienced police constable but tonight he, Percival Oswald, was on his own. It was a brisk, starlit night, with stars scintillating also from all the lamps, a night for a twenty-four-year-old man to revel in.

He was patrolling along a narrow street off Ealing Broadway, past some small shops, one of them with an *Antiques* notice above the door, although to most passers-by the stock seemed a mass of old junk. The street stretched out for a long way, being in one of the older parts of Ealing which had become one of London's high-class inner suburbs. On the other side of the road, Oswald saw a shadow on the wall of the shop, thrown by something in the way of a single, shadeless light bulb which burned during the hours of darkness.

As Oswald watched, the shadow moved. Oswald's heart lurched.

He did not cross the road. *"Do nothing at first to alarm the suspect"* had become a rule of thumb. The shadow kept moving until he was sure someone was there. Of course it could be feathers or something stirred by a draught. He walked on towards a service alley and turned down this. There was a stage when he should use his walkie-talkie to call assistance, but he didn't want to bring a patrol car here unless he was sure of the need.

He counted the number of arch-shaped roofs as he walked quietly along the path, came to the sixth — and tried the back gate. It was unlocked. Now, heart beating faster, he walked along a path with a big shed on one side, glass sides reflecting the light in the sky; it might be a greenhouse. The house was typical of its period, with a single-storey kitchen and scullery jutting out from the main building; the back door would be near the corner made by the two walls. No light showed as he neared the door and for the first time he shone his torch, the modern equivalent of the bull's-eye.

The door was open!

Now his heart began to race, for there could no longer be any doubt; and this was the moment when he should send for help. He pulled up the built-in aerial of his little radio, and as he did so, before switching it on, he heard a rustle behind him.

He swung round.

A man was only a yard away, arm up-raised and weapon in it, already on its way down.

Oswald didn't dodge, didn't back away but simply kicked forward with his left foot, as high as he could. He caught the other in the groin. An anguished gasp of

34

sound came as the man doubled up, and the weapon clattered to the concrete path. There was no more risk from this man, Oswald thought, but if another was inside he might have heard that clattering.

Another phrase hammered into him by a wise old sergeant flashed into his mind.

"Never take a chance unless you have to. Don't just think it's okay. Be certain."

He went forward and grabbed the man who was still doubled up, pushed him upright and then struck him on the chin. The man went back, log-like, banged against the wall and fell. Oswald, one hand at his radio, turned towards the door and at that moment it opened wide and a second man sprang at him.

Oswald repeated his defensive tactics, with exactly the same result, except that this man fell helplessly to one side and on to the ground, twitching his legs as if in anguish. And so he might be, Oswald thought. He switched on the radio, and when he was answered, reported quite calmly.

"You'll have a car within three minutes," Information from the Yard promised him. "Don't let them get away."

"No, sir," Oswald promised.

He was not only very calm, but highly pleased with himself. It was hardly credible that such a thing could have happened on his first solitary patrol, but there were the two men in front of him. He could almost hear that wise old sergeant. "There's just one place to hit or kick for. If you can make it you won't have any trouble." Again he had demonstrated time and time again on a dummy.

On this, his first encounter, Oswald had carried out these instructions to the letter, and they had worked. My God! How they had worked! Although he stood in the middle of the path, narrowing any spot where either man could try to escape, there was no need at all. The men were no longer writhing but they were still on the ground when a car sounded. A car door closed, footsteps echoed clearly along the service alley and along this garden path.

"Now be careful," Oswald warned himself. "Don't talk too much, just play it cool. How do they know it's my first time out?" And he added: "And if they did, why should they care?"

A man approached: "Any trouble?" he

asked, and then saw the two men, and whistled. "Plenty of trouble. Been inside yet?"

"No," Oswald answered. "There was a chance there'd be another, I thought I'd better stay put."

"Couldn't be more right," the patrol car officer said. "I'll take a look around."

He went in with another newcomer while Oswald still stood guard. He was rueful and disappointed, for he wanted to go inside, but he accepted the situation philosophically, while still more men came to take care of his prisoners.

That was at a quarter to three.

That was the moment when, in those witching hours, a pretty girl lay sleeping and a man stood, holding a pillow in his hands, at the side of her single bed. They were in a house less than a hundred yards from the scene of Oswald's triumph.

*   *   *

The girl's name was Rosamund.

The man's name was Wells — David Wells.

They were — or they had been — lovers.

They had made love this night.

He had taken her in all her eagerness, with thought of killing her in his mind. In a way it had been horrible but in another, strangely exciting, increasing his passion and desire.

Now, while she slept, he had dressed and was standing over her.

He *had* to kill her or else face ruin, tragedy, the despair of his wife, the mute hurt of his three children. And he could not face these things.

He had promised Rosamund that he would divorce his wife and marry her, Rosamund, but he had known he could never go through with it. He was sure that if he didn't, then she, Rosamund would go to Ellen and tell her about them, and the hurt would be as great to Ellen as if he were to tell her himself.

These things and many others passed through his mind as he stood above Rosamund.

He had to kill her, *had* to. And it was her own fault, she shouldn't have insisted on divorce and marriage. He hadn't thought she would, hadn't dreamed of it. When he had first come here, to her flat, he had told her he was married. She had talked of love in a permissive society, of wanting only that part of his life he could spare from his wife, but as the days had passed he had come to realise that she did not mean what she said.

She stirred.

He clutched the pillow more tightly.

She settled again, only her head turning to one side. She was flushed, deepening her prettiness into beauty. She had a smooth complexion, without serious blemish, and her dark hair was drawn loosely back from her forehead and caught with a ribbon at the nape of the neck. It made her look so young, almost like a schoolgirl. Well, she was young, twenty-two. And he was thirty-one.

She had such beautiful shoulders, so milky white. And in her sleep she seemed to smile.

He *had* to kill her.

He hadn't, yet; he had committed no crime, for it was no crime in the eyes of the law to commit adultery while seducing a young woman. He would commit no crime until he lowered that pillow and began to smother her.

He *had* to.

She had been so adamant about what he must do, and had used the one argument which had silenced him as it had silenced countless married men before him: she was pregnant with his child.

Once she went to Ellen and told her that there could be no going back. Ellen would divorce him, he had no doubt of that, but it would break her heart: and the children's. And there was another thing: he really could not afford it. He earned less than forty pounds a week as an accountant with a firm in the City of London, and was never likely to earn much more. Rosamund wouldn't be able to work with a baby on the way, and Ellen, with three children under seven, couldn't leave the home. It was utterly hopeless, and the only way out was to kill Rosamund.

Murder her.

She stirred again, more gently even than before.

It was easy to imagine her body beneath the sheet and blanket, easy to remember their passion. Once, he had been oblivious of all else when with her, but of late it had been more like being with Ellen, Ellen who felt no joy and knew no ecstasy but suffered him, turning his love into lust. He could go back in his thoughts to the time when he and Ellen had lain together, in the grass in a little woodland on Ealing Common. At that time too she had "suffered" him, but he had been too young to realise that this was not enough. Yet he had felt committed, and they had gone together for two years before getting married. The strange thing was she so loved having babies; the only time she looked less than plain was when she was with child. And she loved them as babies, too, but was less patient and less loving when they began to walk and talk.

It wasn't any use thinking back.

He had to act, now.

He *had* to murder Rosamund because there was no way of living a peaceful fear-free life with her alive, and because, alive she would so hurt Ellen and the children. He knew the risks. When he had been on his way here he had calculated them. He might be caught, of course, but why should he be? It certainly wasn't inevitable. They seldom went out together. It was his fear that Ellen might see them together that had forced this issue of marriage; that, and the baby. Of course there was risk, but this was a big old house, let off in bed-sitting rooms. Each bed-sitter had its own door to the landings, there was only the communal front door, and it was remarkable how seldom he met anyone on the stairs. There was so much coming and going; some of the girls had different boy-friends every night of the week! And he had always cycled here, never walked; cyclists were less noticed than pedestrians, and there was a spot outside the house where his old bicycle was chained now.

He must get it over.

He must not delay, or he would lose the chance.

Rosamund stirred again and lay on her back, those creamy-textured shoulders so beautiful.

He drew in a deep breath, lowered the pillow, then thrust it over her face and pressed down with all his might. As she began a swift and awful struggle for life he placed his right knee on her stomach so that only her legs could thrash and her chest heave, fighting desperately for the air which was not there.

Soon, her struggling stopped.

He did not move for a long time; a very long time, for he had to be absolutely sure. At last he was. At last he eased off the pressure, but left the pillow over her face and shoulders. He felt her pulse, which was still. He pulled on some thin cycling gloves, and opened the door. He had been so careful not to touch a thing tonight, Rosamund had done everything for him, everything.

He turned his back on her and opened the door; listened, but heard no sound. He went out and closed the door with the slightest of clicks, then went down the stairs which had a strip of coconut matting which deadened all but the loudest of footsteps. At the street door he hesitated again, then opened it and stepped outside. He had done this dozens of times but never before had he been frightened of being seen.

No one was in sight.

His bicycle was still chained to the rails.

He unlocked the padlock, making only a little noise, and cycled off, wheels purring, chain whispering, tyres silent on the smooth-topped road. Now and again a loose mudguard rattled. He turned out of Leith Avenue, into Acacia Road, then into the long narrow Cardiff Street which led to the main road close to the Ealing Town Hall. As he drew near the end of the street he saw two cars with their lights on, and then saw the lighted "Police" sign and his heart nearly turned over, one foot actually slipped off a pedal. Men were coming out of a service road, and he thought that some were handcuffed.

He hated the thought of passing, for policemen had such cat's eyes, and noticed so much that ordinary people wouldn't see. But he must not turn back for they would have seen him by now. He gritted his teeth, kept his head down and went on. If they stopped him, if they even took a good look at him, he was finished.

* * *

Police Constable Oswald saw the cyclist.

The rule book and the sergeant alike said that a strange man or men moving about in the small hours could justifiably be stopped and questioned; ninety times out of a hundred they would be innocent of all crimes, but the hundredth time the man would be fresh from a "job".

But he was feeling very much put out.

44

He had been left outside since the men from the station had arrived, and the sergeant in charge had virtually ignored his existence. (It did not occur to him that the sergeant was deliberately making sure he didn't get a swollen head on his first night on duty alone.) And he was cold. Although he did not realise it, he was suffering from a delayed action shock. Whatever the causes, he watched the cars drive off with *his* prisoners, saw lights on as the patrol men and others from the Division searched the antique shop, and looked at the solitary cyclist without moving.

He *ought* to stop him.

He actually took a step forward, belatedly.

Then he sneezed. It took him completely by surprise and he raised his hand swiftly to his face. The cyclist went by, reached the Broadway, turned right and disappeared.

* * *

He sneezed, thought David Wells in choking excitement.

He sneezed, he probably didn't get a good look at me!

45

CHAPTER 4

MORNING REPORTS

"GOOD morning, Commander . . . Good morning. 'Morning, George — great night last night, wasn't it?"

"Very good indeed."

"Good morning, sir."

"Good morning, sergeant."

Gideon made his way in nigh majestic progression up the steps and along the passages of "old" New Scotland Yard. The move to the splendid new modern building was still several months off, and Gideon had not yet adjusted to the fact that a change was in the offing. There was something reassuringly solid about these old premises, and about his own office, with its two windows overlooking the Embankment, the Thames, the London County Hall and Westminster Bridge itself, with its low parapet and its three-lamp standards and the steady flow of traffic.

Two Chief Superintendents were coming

out of Hobbs's office, next door to Gideon's.

"Good morning, Commander. *Very* good show last night, wasn't it?"

"Very."

The other man's face was deeply chasmed as if there were valleys in flesh dried almost to pale leather. He seemed to have the suffering of the ages in his expression and the wisdom, too. He was Superintendent Piluski.

"Good morning, sir."

"Good morning, Superintendent."

Piluski, a Pole by birth, English by training, soft-footed and quick moving, turned to Gideon's door and opened it for him, while the other man, big, bluff Ringall, went on.

"Thanks," Gideon said. "What are you on at the moment?"

"I'm nearly through with the jewel smuggling case," said Piluski. "It's all over bar shouting."

It was a little strange to hear this coloquialism uttered in his near-guttural voice, almost as strange to observe the droll expression on the harp-shaped lips, to become so aware of his dark, deep-set eyes

47

— so dark at eyebrows and lashes, in fact, that it was almost as if he used eye-black.

"Got them all?" asked Gideon.

"I think so." He made the words sound almost "I zink so."

Gideon nodded as he went in, and Piluski closed the door quietly. Gideon glanced at the pile of reports on his desk, saw that the one on new cases was much fuller than usual and was instantly aware of a direct relation between the police night out and the crooks' night out. He pursed his lips in a resigned grimace, and stepped to the window.

This was almost ritual with him and there could hardly have been a better morning. The sun was breaking through the river's mist, which made the surface of the water look as if it were steaming. The nearer part of the bridge and the Embankment were very sharply etched, but the further end of the bridge and even the County Hall were enshrouded in a misty, pearly grey. Along to the right the new skyline of the south bank of the Thames emerged, the square buildings like futuristic designs of concrete and glass; to the left the graceful arches of Waterloo Bridge, the neo-modern structure of the Festival Hall and the mammoth commercial buildings beyond looked stark and real.

He crossed to his desk and sat down, glanced through the files on new cases and saw none, as far as quick opinion could tell, of exceptional importance. Then he looked through the other files, all of investigations in hand. There had been a time when he would have seen the officers in charge of these, but nowadays Hobbs vetted them and only sent through cases which he, Hobbs, felt needed the Commander's personal attention. Gideon could not recall a single instance where Hobbs's judgement had been wrong.

The jewel smuggling case, covering several weeks' work, was indeed at the point of finish: three members of the crew of an English ship which made a run of English and Dutch and Belgian North Sea ports were under arrest, and a jewel merchant in Hatton Garden was about to be charged with receiving.

Gideon pressed a bell for Hobbs, who, for once, didn't come immediately: that meant he was out of the office or on the telephone. Gideon pushed his own three telephones a little further away: one was green and connected to the Yard's exchange, one was grey, the direct line to the Whitehall exchange, one was black: the internal machine with a great variety of buttons. The desk, of highly polished mahogany like the filing cabinets and a table, had some trays fixed to it. *In, Out, Pending.* There was one file in the *Pending* tray. He picked it up, frowning. It was Riddell's latest report.

The door opened and Hobbs came in, as immaculate in a dark grey suit as he had been last night in tails. He showed no sign of having been up too late. Gideon remembered him going off with Penelope, who hadn't come home before he, Gideon, had gone to sleep; but she had been up before he had left this morning.

"Sorry, sir," Hobbs said.

"That's all right." There was a moment's pause, but Hobbs didn't take the opportunity to say who had been on the telephone, so perhaps it hadn't been so urgent after all. "The boys were busy last night, I see."

"And we made a good haul," Hobbs announced.

50

"That's something."

"Eighty-nine burglaries, and fifty-one arrests or arrests-pending already."

"*Very* good!"

"And I've just heard of the best one we've had for months," said Hobbs, with obvious satisfaction. "Two youths were caught at an old antique and junk shop at Ealing. It turns out that over the past months they'd sold a lot of stolen jewels and silver to the dealer. They went back by night to steal it back, and resell to someone else. Now we have plenty on the dealer, and," — Hobbs chuckled — "something like a hundred thousand poundworth of stolen stuff from beneath the floorboards of the shop. They're still counting at Ealing, there might be twice as much when the count is over."

"It was certainly a big night," said Gideon with equal satisfaction. "Who caught the pair?"

"There's an aspect about that that the Press will go to town on," reported Hobbs. "It was a man out on his own for the first time. He was lucky to strike such a case, of course, but he was on top of his job to start with."

"Check on him," Gideon ordered.

Hobbs knew that the other wanted to find a way of giving the police officer a pat on the back without overdoing it. There was no one like George Gideon on the human and personal side of police work; that was why the Ball had gone with such a swing. And he, Hobbs, shared Gideon's pleasure that the police had had much the better of the night's crimes.

"I'll check," Hobbs promised.

"What else is there?" asked Gideon.

"Not much that need worry you," Hobbs assured him. "Except Riddell and Honiwell, who are due here soon — Riddell at eleven o'clock and Honiwell at eleven-thirty."

"Any ideas?" asked Gideon.

"I think Riddell's going to have a very bad patch," Hobbs ventured, "and Honiwell looks as if he's going to have a good one."

"Because of the Jameson woman, do you mean?"

"Yes. He is not a bachelor at heart," observed Hobbs, drily.

Neither of them realised that the remark was of the kind that Gideon had often made over the years; that just as Hobbs had relieved Gideon of much of the routine, so much that was part of Gideon's success with the Yard's staff had rubbed off on Hobbs, whose thinking and attitudes were becoming more like Gideon's every day. Gideon simply nodded.

"What's your thinking about Riddell?" asked Gideon. "I'd forgotten what a wraith of a wife he had until last night."

"He's had a month's holiday which was long overdue, but it doesn't seem to have done him any good," replied Hobbs. "I think he'll want to be taken off the Notting Hill inquiry, and unless you've very strong reasons to keep him on it, I'd let him go. And — " Hobbs hesitated, and seemed to wait for Gideon but when Gideon didn't respond he went on: "I wish there was a way of putting him out to grass, so to speak."

"He can retire whenever he wants to," remarked Gideon.

"From what you saw last night, would you think retirement would be an inducement?" asked Hobbs.

Gideon sat contemplating him very thoughtfully.

Hobbs had been much quicker than he, Gideon, had expected in seeing the importance to many men of a settled and unharassed home or emotional life. He himself had once come close to a complete break with Kate, because he had put his job before the family interest; a policeman had to, there wasn't any way out. The temperament of a man's wife had a great deal to do with this. Some women could stand the long periods alone, the lonely or interrupted nights, the continual interruptions during "office" or duty hours; the pressure drove other women mad.

"No, probably not an inducement," Gideon conceded. "Then what?"

"I can't come up with a single idea," confessed Hobbs.

"We'll both think about it," said Gideon, and he seemed to brace himself. "Well — it's half-past ten, which doesn't give much time. I'd like you here when Honiwell and Riddell come."

"Thank you," Hobbs said, turning to the door; then he paused and looked back. "George, Penny had the thrill of her life last night when she stood in for Kate. She revelled in it."

"I couldn't be more pleased," said Gideon. He resisted the temptation to ask Hobbs how things were between him and Penelope, and when the door closed he sat back and actually laughed at himself. All he could think about was the emotional life of his men, and he was beginning to forget how many *were* happily married — or at least contentedly. Piluski, for instance; Chief Superintendent Lemaitre, once in Hobb's position as his chief *aide*. Scott-Marle. He himself! Oh, there were dozens. It was always the same; one was more aware of weakness than of strength, of woes and worries than happiness and pleasures.

He dialled the typing pool.

"Send someone to me right away," he ordered.

He knew perfectly well that he hoped that Sabrina Sale would come, but instead it was a long, leggy girl in her early twenties to whom he dictated with little confidence. But she took everything down at speed, he had to say that for her. He was still dictating at a minute to eleven, when Riddell was due.

At last he finished and sent the girl away.

It was already two minutes after eleven; Hobbs probably knew he was busy and was keeping Riddell in his office. So, Gideon rang the buzzer, and immediately Hobbs appeared at the door.

"No Riddell?" asked Gideon.

"No sign of or word from him," answered Hobbs. "And he hasn't been in this morning. He knew last night that he was due here, because he mentioned it."

"Well," Gideon said, "it's not like him to be late. We'll give him ten minutes before we find out where he is."

* * *

Chief Detective Superintendent Thomas Riddell was at Notting Hill Gate.

He had been there since ten o'clock, when a call from Division had reached him not at the Yard but at his own house, in Wembley.

And he felt sick.

In the heart of his Division there lived thousands of Pakistanis, nearly all in overcrowded conditions but most in bearable conditions of hygiene and home life. There was a great deal of happiness here, especially with young children, and many young wives found conditions infinitely better than in the sand-swept villages or the crowded, heat-ridden, fly-ridden cities from which they had come. Perhaps the worst of the situation was not overcrowding but the segregation from neighbours, for there were areas which were exclusively Pakistani, others exclusively Hindu, others again exclusively West Indian. And since each had different cultures, different traditions and different habits, it was difficult for them to mix.

The West Indians — mainly Jamaicans — and in fact most Negroes, found it easier to mix with the ordinary Londoner than with the Pakistanis and Indians. They, like the whites, often felt a kind of uneasiness at close proximity with the Asian race, and there was mutual suspicion based on habitual mistrust rather than any specific reasons.

Crime throve in the area, there was some drug addiction and drug trafficking, a great deal of petty larceny, particularly thefts from cars and pocket picking and bag snatching, mostly within the racial groups. But perhaps the worst crime of all was a "civil", not a criminal offence: overcrowding, letting and sub-letting houses and flats at exorbitant rents.

Riddell had been checking this for a long time.

In the beginning he had been objective enough, although from that beginning he had known he was out of sympathy with all coloured people, and his emotions always responded to political calls to "Keep Britain white". Gradually his prejudices had grown too strong for him, as Gideon knew.

But he was very deeply involved.

He knew that there were whole families, husband, wife — sometimes two wives — and several children living in one room; and many of these terraced houses, once so white and attractive but now dilapidated even on the outside, had a dozen rooms. He knew of houses in which over a hundred human beings shared perhaps three bathrooms and, when the plumbing worked, three water-closets. There was always an odour, and the aroma of spices and smell of unfamiliar vegetables and meats added to this. It had been a long time before Riddell could see the people here as human beings; until in fact he had found the one girl, he had seen them all as "creatures".

Too often, he still did.

But not now, not at this minute, while Gideon and Hobbs were waiting for him. He had completely forgotten the appointment. He was standing, bent forward, with a huge beam across his shoulders, a sloping beam. Two men, taller than he, one a Negro, one a cockney, were on his right; a shorter man, another on his knees and one with a huge steel rod which he was using as a lever, were on his left. Just behind them yet another man was calling:

"*Heave!*" They heaved. "*Heave!*" They heaved. "*Heave!*"

Every muscle in Riddell's body was stretched, every vein in his neck and forehead stood out, and it was the same with all the others.

"*Heave!*" They heaved. "*Heave!*" They heaved.

They raised the beam a little higher, every time, off the bodies of three young children they knew to be beneath the rubble.

CHAPTER 5

COLLAPSE

THE house, one of a terrace of eleven, had collapsed before Riddell had arrived. Divisional police and firemen had been here, although no fire had started. Gas and electricity engineers had turned the supplies off at the main but there was a heavy smell of gas over the street — Long Street, W.7. The police and Fire Brigade had cordoned off the area, then evacuated the residents, and Riddell had been on the spot as that was being done.

He could recall a Divisional detective sergeant say in an unbelieving voice: "My God, there can't be more!"

But there were more. In a steady stream, men, women and a host of children were shepherded out of the neighbouring house, and that exodus continued long after the first (damaged) house had been emptied; or so the police had thought. Riddell had watched as policemen and women, some of them coloured, and firemen, some of them coloured, had escorted the fugitives out. Long Street was a narrow thoroughfare with a road at one end, and blocked at the other by an old railway embankment. It also backed on to a railway cutting, too, and there were a few houses at either end in cul-de-sacs which also ended at the cutting. Beyond the street in the other direction houses in neo-Georgian style and in late Victorian style stretched out in a maze of streets.

In one block of streets was an old church, long since condemned, but kept in reasonable condition so that it could be used for clubs and meetings places for the new population. It was used only occasionally. This morning the doors had been opened wide and the refugees were being ushered into it, while emergency meals and clinics were rushed into service.

Riddell was aware of all this.

Sickened by what he had seen, he had gone back to Long Street and talked to the Fire Brigade chief who was directing salvage and rescue work. By that time Civil Defence crews were in action, and men used to breaking and collapsing walls were moving cautiously about the rubble of the middle house in the street, the one which had collapsed.

One man had appeared at the doorway, alarm vivid in his face.

"We need some volunteers," he called. "Some kids are under the rubble." There was a moment's pause before he went on: "It's bloody dangerous. Two floors could collapse on us."

Now, Riddell was beneath those two floors.

Now, the fireman in charge was calling: "Heave!" And they heaved. "Heave!" And they heaved. There was a creaking and groaning of wood and some falling rubble; somewhere, water was splashing. Dust was thick everywhere. Daylight came through a gaping hole in the roof and in one wall. There was a sickening stench of gas. Now and again a sharp crack came, of an impending fall. If the rest of the house did fall in there would be little help for the straining men.

"Heave!" And they heaved.

Suddenly, a child began to cry.

It was not a wail nor a scream, it was more a whimpering and it came from the rubble just beyond them. A man swore. Another, very small, in fireman's uniform and wearing a steel helmet, was squeezing himself between the beam and the rubble, and clearing away the bricks by hand. There was no room for anyone else.

Riddell felt as if his back would break.

"Heave!" And they heaved as they had never heaved before.

The child went on crying and the strong men bore their burden, and the fireman pulled away brick after brick. At last the beam was high enough for a second man to crawl beneath and help to clear a way, also brick by brick, towards the buried children.

* * *

Gideon looked at the watch on his big wrist with the dark hairs on the wrist and forearm as well as the backs of the fingers. It was twenty minutes past eleven, Honiwell was due in a few minutes and there was still no sign of Riddell. Gideon, although telling himself there must be a good reason, was exasperated; there was never enough time, and he had a feeling that he had not given the racial problem enough concentrated thought. If he had, he might understand Riddell more.

He buzzed for Hobbs, who came in almost at once.

"Any word?" he asked.

"No," said Hobbs. "Every call that comes I expect to be from Riddell. Instead — "

"It's someone to tell us what a great success it was last night," interpolated Gideon sourly. "The Commissioner was positively enthusiastic when he telephoned."

"He quite let his hair down," Hobbs approved.

He broke off when Gideon's Yard exchange telephone bell ran, and Gideon turned, stretched out and picked it up. Outside, an ambulance bell rang; outside, Big Ben began to strike his sonorous hour; outside, traffic was fast and noisy along the Embankment.

"Gideon," said Gideon. "Who? . . . Yes, put him through." "Extension" he breathed to Hobbs who vanished into his own room. This was the Division which included Notting Hill, and the operator had said that it was very urgent; Divisions did not say that to Gideon unless it was so.

"Saxby," a man announced. "Commander Gideon, *at once*."

"What is it, Mark?" asked Gideon

quietly, for the tension in the other's voice was unmistakable.

"George," said Saxby, with a familiarity bridging the years, "a house has collapsed in Long Street, Notting Hill. It looks as if a whole terrace might fall. Most of the occupants have been evacuated, over a thousand from *eleven* houses. Three children are buried beneath the rubble. Riddell's helping to stop a wall from falling on them. I doubt if he'll get out alive."

Gideon felt as cold as ice. The whole picture came over so vividly, and he could almost see Riddell's face, as it had been last night, haunted by what he had discovered and by what he was experiencing.

"I'll come over," Gideon said quietly. "Who's been told?"

"Presumably the Ministry of Housing and the Home Office. The Fire Service is present in strength."

There was a nagging question in Gideon's mind: why hadn't he been told before? If the Fire Service was in strength, some time must have elapsed. But compared with what had happened, that was trifling — except that time saved could mean lives saved.

"I'll come over," he repeated.

"I hoped you would. Ambulances are standing by."

"Good. How weak are the remaining walls?"

"So weak it looks as if a high wind would blow them over," answered Saxby. "God knows what's been going on to bring this about. This has all the makings of a major disaster. I hate to say it, but — " He paused, and Gideon heard noises in the background, raised in excitement if not in alarm, and cold dread filled him for fear that those walls had collapsed. The voices continued, closer, still full of excitement, and Saxby kept calling out: "What? . . . Where? . . . How big?" and similar questions. Gideon began to think the Divisional man had forgotten him, but suddenly Saxby boomed into his ear:

"George! A mob's after the landlord. They're screaming 'lynch him'."

* * *

On this instant there was born a new and major task for the police, for George Gideon. And now, on this very instant, he realised that he knew nothing like enough.

66

He had to learn more very quickly, so that he could decide what action to recommend. As these thoughts flashed into his mind the communicating door from Hobbs's room opened and Hobbs came in with his usual controlled briskness.

"You handle this landlord threat," Gideon ordered. "Use Rollo and Piluski if they're free, and make sure they have all the help they need. Have the neighbouring Divisions standing by and alert the Flying Squad. We want that landlord both to save his neck and — " He broke off, with a savage grin. "Well, we want him. Just concentrate on that."

Hobbs said one word: "Honiwell."

Gideon hesitated for a second.

"Have him fix a car for me with a driver, and we can talk on the way to Notting Hill. I'll talk to the Commissioner now." Gideon knew that he should go through the Assistant Commissioner, but there simply wasn't time.

Hobbs, already at the door, said: "Donaldson isn't in."

"Thank God for that!" Gideon was already dialling the Commissioner's number. As it rang and he forced himself to wait patiently, he felt tension so great that it set his teeth on edge and stiffened his stomach muscles. Scott-Marle wasn't in his office, it seemed, and this was hardly a subject about which to leave a message. He forced himself to wait for at least two minutes, and then rang off.

For the moment, he was nonplussed.

He kept imagining Riddell, helping to hold up that wall, Riddell, who in one way was going to pieces. And he kept picturing a mob howling after the landlord. The Home Office had to be told through the Yard even though it already knew. Alec — that was it — Alec could keep trying for the Commissioner when he, Gideon, had left.

The door opened and Scott-Marle came in.

A pale-grey suit seemed to emphasise his gauntness, and something in his mood put abruptness into his manner. He closed the door on footsteps in the passage and, not far off, the sound of a man laughing.

"Good morning, sir," Gideon said.

" 'Morning. What's this at Notting Hill?" Scott-Marle demanded.

"Ugly wall collapse, with Riddell trying

to help hold it up, apparently," Gideon answered. "I'm going over at once. Hobbs will keep on top of things here. Did you hear that a mob is after the landlord?"

"No," Scott-Marle replied. "I had a vague call from the Home Office." He paused as Gideon ruffled through some papers on his desk and went on: "What's this about Riddell?"

Gideon gave him the essence of the story, even etching in Riddell's personal attitude and his, Gideon's, doubts about what to do over his future. He leaned against the desk, a file in his hand. There was some quality in Scott-Marle which brought out the best in him.

At last, he stopped. In his mind there was a different kind of pressure: he ought to be on his way, for God knew what was happening at Long Street. Another thought followed fast upon that. There wasn't anything he could do if he got there, except show everyone how important the disaster was to the Yard.

Scott-Marle's eyes looked ice-cold.

"How much of this have you told Mr. Donaldson in the past?"

"Everything, except my doubts after

seeing Riddell last night," Gideon answered. "He's not in this morning, so I've not been able to tell him about this."

"He won't be in for several days," Scott-Marle told Gideon, and then added right out of the blue: "George, you should be the Assistant Commissioner for Crime. You must know that."

He left the words hanging, as it were, in mid-air; a kind of challenge and the very last thing Gideon wanted to cope with this morning. But this *was* Scott-Marle, who did not say anything out of the blue unless he had already given it a great deal of thought. Slowly he relaxed. A grim smile played about his mouth, and he went on: "Ponder what I've said in the knowledge that Mr. Donaldson will be leaving at the end of the year. He told me so last night."

That, in its way, was an even greater surprise; and all Gideon could find to say was: "I'll ponder, sir." He held the file out, and Scott-Marle's fingers tightened on to the other end so that for a moment both of them held it. "This is the file on the situation which led to the Notting Hill Gate disaster and could lead to others."

"The racial situation, you mean?"

"Yes."

Scott-Marle took the file. The ice seemed back in his eyes, the momentary warmth of that "George" was gone. One thing was absolutely certain about this man: the Yard, his job, came remorselessly first.

"It doesn't seem very full."

"It isn't full enough," Gideon said. "I've been inclined to let it slide."

Scott-Marle did not even glance away from Gideon, who was increasingly and sickeningly aware of the fact that he should have given much more attention to the dangers in the immigration problems, not simply dealt with the actual crimes which had emerged from it, but gone to the heart. He shouldn't have left Riddell in charge for so long, and should have taken the chance to put in a powerful team during Riddell's holiday, instead of keeping the investigation ticking over. It passed through his mind that this report had been on the Assistant Commissioner's desk several times but Donaldson had made only one comment on each occasion: "*Keep me informed.*" But he, Gideon, could and should have pushed; instead, he had waited for a catastrophe to shock him into action.

"Well, we can't let it slide any longer," Scott-Marle observed at last. "Come and see me as soon as you're back."

"Right," said Gideon, and as Scott-Marle turned towards the door, the folder now under his arm, he went on in an almost casual way: "One other thing while you're here, sir."

Scott-Marle could pivot about like a youth, and did so.

"Yes?"

"The Entwhistle case," Gideon said, and paused.

"The man you think might have been wrongly imprisoned — yes." Scott-Marle waited. He could have heard of this only twice, and each time briefly, over the past year but Gideon was sure that he had the details at his fingertips.

"I'd like to reopen the case, sir. We've found a man who knew Entwhistle's wife, and was undoubtedly her lover. There are a lot of details we haven't discovered yet but I think the time has come to start asking the man a few questions. And also, to ask Entwhistle some questions, which will raise *his* hopes. Once we do either, of course, the fact that we're reconsidering the case will come out. And it will be sensational. He's been in prison for over two years, already."

Scott-Marle considered before asking quietly: "Who is on the case?"

"Honiwell. The last man in the world to make a report unless he was absolutely sure of himself."

"Yes," Scott-Marle said. "Yes. You'd better handle it as you think fit. Let me know how it goes, but don't leave it hanging fire any longer."

"Thank you, sir," Gideon said.

This time, Scott-Marle went out, the door opening and closing on footsteps just outside. After allowing his chief time to reach the lifts to his office, Gideon went after him. Honiwell would wonder what had happened and Saxby what the blazes was delaying him. Neither greatly mattered. Those ten minutes or so with Scott-Marle had covered a great deal of ground and they showed more vividly than ever the Commissioner's belief in him.

Too vividly? wondered Gideon.

The question of the Assistant Commissionership had been raised before. He had rejected the offer, convinced that he was in the right job, and would stay there for the rest of his police service. But he felt sure this time, Scott-Marle would push much harder to make him accept. There had been a succession of Assistant Commissioners in recent years, none of them really satisfactory, but Donaldson was by far the worst.

Gideon went down the stone steps in a hurry, to find Honiwell at the foot of the steps by a car with a peak-capped driver by the open door.

"In you get," said Gideon, and in a few seconds they were turning out of the gates on the Embankment side, heading for Notting Hill.

CHAPTER 6

RESCUE EFFORT

The man who seemed to have been standing behind Riddell and the others, saying "Heave!" at regular intervals, had not spoken for at least a minute. Now, he said: "Hold it." Riddell, sweat pouring down his face and his back, waist and thighs feeling as if they would break, went still; the weight seemed greater and he felt that he must give way.

The child was whimpering now; and therefore, alive.

Riddell swivelled his gaze towards the left and saw what was happening; two men were pushing a steel girder beneath the beam, to take the weight, while the little man who had been squeezing through was now on the other side, moving bricks with a curiously disciplined speed and precision.

The man behind said: "Slow down with that bar, Jimmy."

The little man growled: "What the hell!"

"You don't want the floor to go, do you?"

God, thought Riddell, there was even danger of that.

Some rubble fell. He held his breath, and his heart began to pound. The men pushing at the beam paused, and so did Jimmy. In the following hush, they could hear only the sound of their breathing. The falling stopped, and the man out of sight spoke again.

"They're shoring the floor up, but take it easy." There was a pause. "Now try again — you chaps keep still."

The bar was pushed slowly, agonisingly slowly, beneath the beam. Jimmy moved more bricks. The whimpering seemed to become more shrill, angry. Riddell felt an easing of the pressure on his shoulders as the beam was raised. It was as if all the blood and strength had drained out of his body. But the weight *was* easing. A hand rested on his shoulder, a voice sounded in his ear.

"Squeeze out, sir — I'll take over."

Slowly, agonisingly slowly, every muscle in his body groaning, Riddell backed away and another, fresh-looking man, a fireman, slid into his place but stood inches higher. It looked as if the beam was being held by the bar. Three men were clearing away the rubble with surprising speed but nevertheless with deliberation. Riddell, the weight gone, staggered and thought he would fall; he was terrified of what would follow if he thudded down. Suddenly he felt strong arms round his waist.

"Take it easy, sir. I'll keep you on your feet." There was a pause. "Now back a little, not too much at a time." Step by step Riddell was led out of this chamber. Dazedly he became aware of the staircase, still standing but open to the skies. He saw the crowd of policemen, firemen, newspaper photographers and reporters, all of them covered with dust, all staring.

He went down a step. A board groaned.

"It's all right," his helper said. "The staircase is supported."

Riddell went down another step as a man in the street said as if with anger: "The whole bloody lot could cave in, you can't support that ruin." It wasn't frightening to Riddell any more, for he was only a few feet away from the top of a pile of rubbish: if it came to a point he could jump. The man behind him said: "All right, sir." A uniformed constable came, treading on bricks and plaster and stirring up little clouds of dust. He put out a steadying arm.

"This way, sir. There's a first-aid post over here."

Why should he need a first-aid post?

"It's Riddell," a newspaperman exclaimed excitedly.

"Hold it!" cried a photographer.

"Superintendent Riddell," called out another newspaperman.

"Just one more, sir." Flash went his camera: flash, flash, flash.

"Is it true there are some children buried along there?"

"Any signs of life?"

"How many workers up there, sir?"

Questions, questions, questions; and Riddell, usually very publicity conscious, did not answer one. He ached abominably, he was parched, he was sweating, he could hardly hear. A path opened in the crowd, the cameras ceased clicking and flashing. He was led into one of the houses opposite, where there was a stench he didn't like but at least no loose bricks, no falling walls. A door was open on the right. Inside were some nurses, a policeman, two women in a greenish uniform and the badge of the Women's Voluntary Services who were at a table with an array of white cups and saucers, plates of sandwiches, two big bright urns, presumably one of tea and one of coffee.

And there were chairs.

There was a mirror, too. He saw a big scratch across his forehead, where dust had dried on oozing blood, and other scratches; he looked at death's door. The thought made him give a fierce grin, and a woman asked:

"Tea or coffee?"

"Tea," he said.

Tea, more tea, his forehead bathed, his faced washed with unusual tenderness, his jacket shaken nearly clean — in twenty minutes he felt a new man. And three others were brought across, the last one the little fellow who had crawled beneath the beam. He had curly hair covered with chippings of brick and plaster, and merry blue eyes. *And he was smiling broadly.*

Riddell asked hoarsely: "Get those kids?"

"Yes — and all alive, too. They — "

Suddenly there was a roar of cheering from the street, nearly everyone in this room moved swiftly forward towards the window. Two men were coming up the staircase which was now bare to the sky, each carrying a child. A moment later a third man appeared, a child held high on his chest, a curly-haired Pakistani child with huge eyes.

The cheering went on and on.

Ambulances moved up slowly and the children were placed in them, there was more cheering as they moved off. The curly-haired man, coffee in one dirty hand and a sandwich in the other, turned round and looked at Riddell.

"Bloody good job you did."

"*I* did!" gasped Riddell.

"Couldn't have got under that beam if there hadn't been a team of Atlases to hold it up," the curly-haired man declared. "I wonder what my wife will say when she learns she's married to a bloody hero?" He held out his cup for more coffee, and Riddell's thoughts switched for the first time since he had arrived, to his wife and to the emptiness of his home life.

Other men came in, all looking as if they had been covered by rubble, then some newspaper reporters and cameramen arrived in a bunch, flash, click, questions; flash, click, questions. Riddell was jolted out of himself again. There was excitement in this, in the fact that all the rescue team were here together, being photographed. He hadn't dreamed of anything like this when he had come. And there was the deep satisfaction of having saved those children.

A middle-aged reporter approached.

"Congratulations, Superintendent."

Riddell just waved his hands.

"I know you've had all you can take this morning, but if you could answer a few questions we'd all be grateful." In the skilful and anonymous way of newspapermen they had made a circle about him, cutting him off from the others in the rescue team. "You were the only C.I.D. man up there, weren't you?"

"Yes," Riddell said.

"Any special reason for your being on the spot?"

"Yes," Riddell said.

"What?"

"There's been a lot of petty larceny and some major larcenies here, as a result of the overcrowding. Some drug-taking, too. I was checking."

"On your own, Superintendent?"

"The Divisional people were also involved."

"Mr. Riddell," a man called out, "how long has the Yard been inquiring into conditions in this area?"

"Not the conditions as such, but the consequences of them," Riddell corrected.

"Where does the dividing line come, sir?"

"That's a matter of official policy, you'll have to ask someone senior to me," Riddell replied. At least the ordeal hadn't addled his mind.

"Superintendent," called the man who had started to ask the questions, "did you know that a young Pakistani girl died in one of the houses in Long Street a few weeks ago?"

Riddell drew in a deep breath, and said sharply: "Yes."

"Is the Yard inquiring into her death, by any chance?"

Riddell knew that he was in a spot; that he shouldn't have started answering the questions so freely, should have drawn the line earlier. He could and should push this on a superior; he had to answer but the answer had to be phrased in such a way that it did not give too much away.

At last he said: "Yes. We found she died from malnutrition, and we wanted to find out how she came to be here and what led to the malnutrition, how it came about that anyone could die in such circumstances in the middle of London. In one way it's a matter for society and the social services but we want to make sure there is no direct criminal cause."

"Such as a landlord profiteering?"

"That's not an offence, and you know it. And don't put words into my mouth," Riddell rebuked. "My job is simply to make sure there is no cause for a criminal charge."

A uniformed man appeared at the doorway and boomed across the words, the booming reverberating, the words making everyone look round, charging everyone present with a new sense of urgency.

"Clear the house!" came the cry. "Clear the house! The houses on the other side are tottering."

There was a concerted movement towards the speaker and the doorway. He disappeared. Two men picked up the urns, the W.V.S. women began to pack the cups and saucers into a big wicker basket. Several men grabbed sandwiches and began to eat as they went out. Two photographers turned in one direction and climbed on walls to get better pictures. The uniformed man at the doorway called out: "Leave those cups and saucers, and *hurry*." The hamper was full, and the two women carried it between them. By sheer chance, Riddell was at the back of the crowd, and he stood aside for the women to pass.

There was a curious groaning sound.

Someone called out in a piercing whisper: "Hurry!"

The two W.V.S. women began to run, the crockery rattling in the basket. The men with the urns and those ahead of them also began to run. The groaning

84

sound became an ear-splitting roar. A bulge appeared in the wall of a house next to the one already in ruins; another great bulge in the walls of the houses on either side.

"My God!" breathed Riddell. "I've had it."

He couldn't leap forward because the women were in the way. He couldn't go back, there wasn't time. Suddenly, the sky went dark. He caught a glimpse of a mass of brick and rubble, mortar and stone, overhead like a huge, smoking ceiling. He heard a roar like the thunder of an express train at speed. He covered his head with his arms and went down on his knees, huddled up to protect himself as much as he could. One moment it was as if he were suspended: the next, as if the "ceiling" fell on top of him. It came like a wall of solid rock, absolutely flattening him. All the breath was knocked out of his body in a whining gust.

*　*　*

Gideon sat in silence for a few minutes as the driver coped with traffic which was packed sardine-tight. Honiwell looked at the traffic, the pedestrians, Parliament Square, anywhere but at Gideon. At last Gideon stirred out of a reverie mostly about Scott-Marle's clear statement about the Assistant Commissionership.

"Larry," he said to the driver, "tell *Information* to help keep me informed of any new major developments at Notting Hill, but nothing else."

"Very good, sir," the driver replied.

"Now, Matt," Gideon said to Honiwell, "we may not have time to make a job of it before we reach the trouble spot, but we'll finish this afternoon, if we have to. I've a feeling that you think the Entwhistle case is coming to the boil."

"You couldn't be more right," Honiwell agreed.

"The question is, are you?" retorted Gideon.

Honiwell gave a faint smile. He had always been a calm man, and one of rare compassion. There were superintendents, like Rollo, who simply saw their job as a puzzle; people were often ciphers to such men. There were others, like Piluski, who probed deep into the technicalities of a problem, almost as if they plunged into their work to escape. There were fewer, perhaps, like Honiwell, whose compassion — love — for their fellow human beings spread to criminals as well as victims, yet who had a greater ruthlessness in hunting down criminals because they also had a keenly developed sense of right and wrong, as distinct from guilty and not guilty.

"Well, Commander," Honiwell said after a long pause, "I think — I *know* — that I've taken the Entwhistle case as far as it will go without talking to the new suspect, and to Entwhistle himself and — possibly the worst — to his children."

They sat unspeaking for a few seconds, with the throbbing of a bus engine on one side and the throbbing of a lorry engine on the other, cars and taxis a solid phalanx in front of them.

"Why the children ?" asked Gideon.

"The man I now suspect may have visited the Entwhistle house while their father was away," Honiwell said.

"Have you any reason to suspect he did ?" asked Gideon.

"No, sir. Except that it is now established

that this man Greenwood was Mrs. Entwhistle's escort at intervals over a period of more than two years. In that time it is obviously possible that Greenwood went there once or twice. The oldest child, Clive, might well have remembered." When Gideon didn't answer, Honiwell went on patiently: "I know there's no certainty, but if the boy did see him and does remember, then we would have evidence that Greenwood was at the house at least once. We could do with a witness, sir. So far all we've got is circumstantial evidence."

Gideon pursed his lips.

"Hardly enough to reopen the case, Matt."

"I don't know," said Honiwell. "I really don't know. I've talked to the Governor at Dartmoor, to several of the warders, the prison visitors as well as the Rev. Wilkinson, who was here on leave from Nigeria for three weeks. They have all come to the conclusion that Entwhistle is innocent. And I've had all the records put through a sieve, sir — had three men go through them, all different types of men. They all come up with the same opinion. The fact, which weighed so heavily with the jury, on which Golightly built our case, was that Entwhistle was the only man with a motive. There appeared to be no one else. But we now know for certain that there was someone else who might have had a motive, this man Greenwood. It's at least possible that had Golightly discovered this chap at the time the whole case might have gone differently." When Gideon simply nodded, Honiwell went on: "If the boy Clive Entwhistle could swear he'd seen Greenwood, then we'd be in a much stronger position when we went to talk to Entwhistle."

"Yes," Gideon agreed. "I can see that. Matt, as this case appears to me there are three different aspects. First ours: if we reopen it, submit new evidence and recommend a Queen's pardon, the Home Office is going to want to test every possible link. They'll be on our necks like a ton of bricks. The fact that Golightly, the man in charge of prosecution and the investigation has retired and gone to live in Australia won't make any difference; in a way the Yard will be on trial."

Honiwell countered: "We'd be on trial all right if we thought there was a strong possibility of a miscarriage of justice and we didn't push as far as we could go."

"Matt," Gideon said, "we mustn't push until we are absolutely certain in our minds. If we still need evidence on top of such certainty we might have to take a chance, but we — and that really means *I* — have to be convinced. And you have to convince me," he added, wryly. "I've the Commissioner's authority to use my own judgement."

Honiwell's eyes lit up.

"Then we're nearly home!"

"Hold on," protested Gideon. "There are two other aspects I want to talk about. The second is — "

He broke off as a green light showed at the radio telephone. The driver leaned forward and flicked on the sound. Immediately, a voice from *Information* crackled into the car, carrying an unmistakable edge of excitement.

". . . Calling Commander Gideon . . . Commander Gideon, reply please . . . Over."

Gideon stretched over the back of the

seat next to the driver and took the receiver.

"Commander Gideon here," he said. "What is it?"

"The whole row of houses in Long Street, Notting Hill, has collapsed," *Information* stated clearly. "Among the dozen or so people buried is Chief Superintendent Riddell, sir. They're digging in the rubble now."

For a moment, it was as if an icy blast had come into the car: Gideon had never felt such a shock. He had to fight for self-control as he said.

"I'm nearly there. Over and out." He rang off, stretched out and replaced the receiver, then turned and looked squarely at Honiwell, still fighting for self-control. "Matt," he said, "we'll be on the spot in five minutes. Our business will have to wait."

"Yes. I see that," said Honiwell, returning Gideon's gaze with equal frankness. "Entwhistle's been waiting in Dartmoor for three years. He's used to waiting."

CHAPTER 7

MOB

As Gideon's car drew up at the approach to Long Street, a policeman approached with an officious manner and stood squarely in front of the bonnet, as if defying the driver to come an inch further. Sitting with the window open and looking up at a pall of dust which hung over the whole area, Gideon heard him say:

"What's the matter, can't you read? There's a diversion."

The driver got out, saying clearly: "What's the matter, are you blind?" and opened the door for Gideon.

There was a big square here, where houses had been demolished, a huge board announcing a new block of flats to come. On one side were white ambulances, on the other, fire-engines, and behind both, police cars. Two men were carrying a stretcher on which a man lay, obviously unconscious, face pale and wan; his hair was covered with dust and debris.

One man, apparently a young doctor, walked alongside him as they approached an ambulance. Chief Superintendent Saxby, the Divisional Chief, came hurrying up, a big man with a heavy paunch, yet immaculately dressed in brown. He had a big jowl and a thick neck and sloping shoulders, which made him rather like a huge russet pear standing upside down. His hips were unexpectedly narrow and fell away into long, slim legs.

"Good morning, sir."

"Found Riddell?" asked Gideon, and he heard a whisper from his chauffeur to the officious policeman; it sounded like *"Bloody fool."*

"No," Saxby answered. "He's still missing. Two W.V.S. women are, too. We aren't sure any others are under the rubble." He led the way over cables, hoses and some loose bricks, along a street which had been evacuated, to the end of Long Street.

Only one side of what had been the terrace of houses was standing, and firemen and Civil Defence men with some military were moving about piles of rubble, somehow pushing wood beams and metal girders into position to shore up the walls while the rescue work went on.

The street itself was choked with rubble.

At the far end the pile was higher and thicker than anywhere else. Men moved about it, obviously with great care, as if desperately anxious that they should not collapse on any pocket of comparative security beneath. A dozen men were picking up bricks and huge pieces of brickwork, handing these along a chain of helpers, the men bringing up the rear putting the rubble into metal barrows, which were being wheeled away. At least thirty men were on this operation alone.

"Riddell's under that," Saxby announced. "He did an unbelievable job this morning, Commander. There was no need for him to volunteer, but he did like a shot. Saved the lives of three children as a result."

Gideon grunted. Honiwell looked shaken, and could not keep his gaze off the huge pile of bricks.

"What's this about the landlord?" Gideon asked.

Saxby said. "They've holed him up

at the top of a house he operates from. I was there when I heard about Riddell. We've got the mob under control, I think, but — " Saxby shook his head. "If this job gets much bigger I don't know what will happen."

"Where is the mob?" asked Gideon.

"In Lancelot Crescent," answered Saxby.

"Who's in charge?"

"My number two man — Archer."

"You stay here and keep an eye on the rescue work," said Gideon. "I'll go to Lancelot Crescent."

"I'll give you a guide," offered Saxby. "The whole area is like a battlefield this morning." Swinging round, he saw the constable who had blocked their way. "Jeffs! Guide the Commander's driver to Lancelot Crescent, at once."

The man seemed to gulp.

"Very good, sir."

Gideon got in, and Honiwell behind him. In the past few minutes Gideon had forced himself to think objectively, to fight back for Riddell and the others under the rubble, to think of what would happen if the mob Saxby talked about did break through the police cordon and lynch the landlord. That must be stopped at all costs. If there was one such triumph for mob violence with the temper of so many people tense on the race or colour problem, it could lead to attempts to establish mob law, could be disastrous. It didn't matter what had led up to the situation; it now had to be stopped.

The constable was sitting next to the driver.

"First right, first left, then second right," he guided.

Soon they were past the ambulances and the fire-engines but not beyond the evidences of "battle". Throngs of people were in the streets, nearly all of them coloured, although there was a sprinkling of whites. Police were dotted about but if serious trouble developed there simply weren't enough of them to maintain control. At the corner of the last turning, still under the policeman's guidance, two or three men in a group were arguing fiercely, and at the next corner a little Pakistani was being pressed against the wall by two big Jamaicans, while a crowd gathered round. Two policemen came hurrying and one man called:

"Break it up there. Break it up."

The police constable ventured: "That's one of Rataudi's rent collectors."

"Whose?" Gideon demanded, and his voice sounded very loud in the car.

"Rataudi, sir — Mahommet Rataudi. He owns a lot of the places around here."

"Including Long Street?"

"Yes, sir."

"How well do you know the situation?" asked Gideon.

"Pretty well, sir. I've been on this beat for two years." The man, whose helmet kept touching the roof of the car, turned his head; he had a very pale face, sharp and rather ugly features. "It's been going from bad to worse."

"Tell me what you can," ordered Gideon.

"Well, sir." The man twisted bodily round in his seat. "The truth is that more and more immigrants come in and more and more babies are born, and there's just no room for expansion. All the property we're driving through now is tenanted by families who've lived here on and off for years. Mostly white people. *This* area isn't overcrowded and there's a kind of vigilance committee which makes sure there's no racket here."

"Racket?"

"Overcrowding like in the Long Street area, sir. It's terrible along there."

Gideon thought: I should have come to look for myself. I shouldn't have left it to Riddell. Self-reproach didn't help, but he had to exert every possible effort to make sure the situation got no worse; keeping Rataudi safe from this mob was an absolute priority.

"How long have you known about it?" Gideon asked.

"Pretty well since it began, sir. The trouble is . . ." There was a helpless note in the man's voice. *First left now.* It kind of grew up on us, sir. We knew there were plenty of people living in Rataudi's houses but they came from other places overnight. A lot of them were fresh in from Pakistan, couldn't even speak English, beat me at first how they got in. Then it dawned on me and the rest of us that a lot were being smuggled in. Those few the Sussex police caught coming ashore were just the tip of the iceberg, sir. *Second left and over Bayswater Road.* What with adults being smuggled in and babies being born and some people coming from the North and the Midlands, it was like squeezing a quart into a pint pot. A gallon, rather. *Now straight on to the end of this street, that's Lancelot Terrace.*"

For the past ten minutes they had been passing through nearly deserted streets with only a few pedestrians, mothers pushing prams, tradesmen with their vans. Suddenly a crowd of people surged across the road at the end of this street, thirty or forty of them at least; and dozens more followed. Probably one in every three was white, mostly long-haired and young. A roaring sound, of voices, became very loud.

At last the police car turned into Lancelot Crescent.

Here, the houses were in graceful Georgian or neo-Georgian, with big white pillars, tall windows, obviously the homes of prosperous people. But at the far end a cordon of police was struggling to keep a mob of people away from the entrance to a house which stood in its own grounds.

As Gideon wound down his window, a brick was hurled against the window of the house, and it crashed in. Another brick was hurled, striking the wall and breaking into hundreds of pieces which flew over and on to the heads of the crowd. More people, black and white, Pakistani, Negroes and English, were streaming into Lancelot Crescent from other roads which debouched into it. Three youths were standing on the roof of a police car, bellowing, and the words came clearly to Gideon.

"String him up!"

"Murderer!"

"Hang him, hang the swine!"

"Hang him!"

Now more and more bricks were thrown, more glass smashed. The policeman next to the driver looked apprehensively over his shoulder at Gideon, and ventured:

"Should you be here, sir?"

"Yes," Gideon said in a hard voice. "Larry, send for more help. Talk to Mr. Hobbs, tell him we want a detachment of military." He placed his fingers on the handle of the car door.

"George," said Matthew Honiwell, "you shouldn't go yourself."

At that juncture they were behind the thickest part of the crowd, although men, mostly youths, were rushing past them. On the other side of the street two youths yanked open the door of a police car, and then pulled the radiotelephone out of its socket. Larry was calling *Information*, and an answer came clearly into the car.

"More patrol cars and some soldiers are on the way to Lancelot Crescent. Mr. Hobbs is on his way also."

Trust Alec!

"George — " repeated Honiwell. "You shouldn't go." He was already getting out on the other side. "Leave it to me."

Gideon opened his door. A youth, passing, grabbed and tried to slam it back, but that was like trying to bend steel. Gideon got out. The youth, who hardly came up to his shoulder, glared up in defiance which faded when he saw Gideon's face. Gideon placed a hand on his shoulder and spun him round.

"Go back the way you came," he ordered.

"Who are you to tell me what — " the youth began.

Gideon pushed him and he went staggering into another youth who was rushing up to join the crowd. Gideon barred the way between the car and the wall of the garden, while Honiwell, the driver and the policeman stretched out across the road to block the way of the stream of people still coming to join the mob. The shouting and the screaming, the smashing of glass and the breaking of bricks was bedlam, and the three youths on top of the police car were leading the mob, calling:

"Hang him!"

"Hang Rataudi!"

"*String him up, hang him! String him up, hang him!*"

"*Hang Rataudi!*"

"*Hang him!*"

Now Gideon was facing six or seven youths, all white-skinned, who were obviously going to rush him, but he lunged forward first, and the very sight of him made one youth stagger back and another stumble. The three policemen in the road had linked arms and were forcing the crowd back. But so many more were streaming towards the spot that they could not be held back for long.

Suddenly, two cars turned into the road, and a moment later, two jeeps. As police sprang out of the cars, young troops jumped down from the jeeps and there was nothing more to worry from this side.

Gideon turned round to the refrain of:

"Hang him, hang him, hang the swine, hang him!"

Inside the house policemen were at the windows, trying to prevent the mob from climbing in. At the porch other policemen seemed to have disappeared, and the mob was hurling themselves against the door. Gideon simply strode into them from behind, grabbing men right and left and thrusting them behind him. They were all taken so much by surprise that none put up serious resistance. Sooner than he had expected, Gideon was at the foot of the steps which led up to the porch, and at the same instance, Honiwell appeared on the other side.

"You take one, I'll take the next,"

Gideon said. He gripped a man by the waist and lifted him off his feet and pushed him over into the little basement area, and Honiwell did the same but dropped his man over the steps and wall onto the corner pavement. Up in the porch eight or nine youths, white and black and pale brown, were hurling themselves at the door, unaware of what was going on behind them.

Gideon took another man, Honiwell yet another, but before they could start again the door crashed in and every one of the crowd on the porch was pitched into the hall.

Thrust back against the wall inside was a policeman in uniform, and at the foot of the stairs was another. No one could have the slightest doubt that each of these men was frightened.

CHAPTER 8

NO PAUSE

THE door lay open. The men who had pushed it, two big Negroes, a Pakistani with powerful shoulders and a white youth with a spade jaw and huge, clenched hands, all recoiled. A policeman came staggering from the front room, two more assailants were hurling themselves at him. All of this was crystal clear to Gideon as he thrust a man behind him.

He drew in a deep, searing breath, and bellowed: "Stop this. *Stop it!*" He hurtled forward, pushing two startled Negroes aside, and strode to the stairs, Honiwell close behind him. "The next man who uses violence will be put under arrest *now!*" He jumped up two stairs and glowered about him, and he looked enormous, towering over everyone including Honiwell. "Now! Out of the house all of you!"

One man shouted: "Get him!" and rushed forward.

Honiwell, close to the wall, grabbed him round the waist. The policeman who had looked so scared only seconds ago pulled out a pair of handcuffs and, with near sleight of hand, slid them over the wrist of the man Honiwell was holding. There was a sudden, startled pause before Gideon demanded:

"Any more for arrest?"

A young soldier appeared on the porch, two more just behind him. The roaring and the chanting stopped. More policemen and soldiers appeared and Gideon beckoned Honiwell and turned to go upstairs. On the first landing two uniformed policemen stood on guard.

"Where's Rataudi?" demanded Gideon.

"One floor up, sir," a policeman said.

"Thanks." Gideon strode along another passage and then up a narrower flight of stairs, at the top of which stood a solitary policeman. "Which room?" asked Gideon.

The policeman pointed to one of two doors.

"This, sir."

Gideon nodded, and went to the painted door and rapped on the solid wood. There was no immediate answer. Partly because he was up here, partly because the police and military had taken over, it was very quiet. Honiwell's voice, on the landing below, was hushed. And compared with the houses in Long Street, this house was a palace. The walls were freshly painted, some fine prints and two maps of West Pakistan were on the walls, the carpet was thick-piled.

Gideon rapped again: "Open," he called, "in the name of the law."

It was a long time since Gideon had taken such an active part in any case, and now that the physical exertion was over he felt not only breathless but aware of a kind of novelty, of unfamiliarity. He might almost be a Chief Inspector again or a newly-promoted superintendent.

"Mr. Rataudi," he called.

The door opened a few inches, on a chain. A man's face appeared on a level with Gideon's chin, a dark face, and narrow. The forehead was so high he looked almost deformed.

"I am a police officer," Gideon stated firmly. "Let me in, Mr. Rataudi." He heard a movement behind him, glanced round and saw a policeman in uniform. "Don't waste time."

The policeman said: "Mr. Archer's compliments, sir. Everything's now under control."

Gideon nodded. Rataudi unfastened the chain and stood aside.

Gideon was aware of several things at once. This was the first he had heard from Archer, Saxby's second in command, and he hadn't yet seen the man; that this Rataudi looked no more than twenty-six or seven; that the room was draped in brightly coloured cottons; that there were four single beds, each without a pillow but stacked with cushions; and that more cushions were spread about the floor, itself covered with a rich-looking carpet. The windows were covered with heavy curtains, the light came from a centre lamp in the ceiling and from lamps at the walls. On a low table stood a lamp, burning and giving off the smoke of a slightly perfumed incense.

Only the young man was in the room.

Gideon said gruffly: "Well, you're safe for the time being."

Rataudi inclined his head, and clasped

long, pale hands together, as if in prayer.

"I am grateful. Very grateful." His English was good but had a faint lilt, rather like Welsh. "Who are you, please?"

"I am Commander Gideon, of Scotland Yard."

"*Commander* Gideon." The man looked astonished. "I have heard of you, you are very famous. I am doubly grateful."

"Mr. Rataudi," Gideon said, "a crowd of people who think you are responsible for the disaster in Long Street this morning wanted to take the law into their own hands. My job is to see that the law is carried out. I shall need to ask you a lot of questions and would like you to come with me to Scotland Yard. You may, of course, have a lawyer present." He paused, and then added: "I haven't much time. Will you come with me?"

Rataudi answered: "It will be my willing duty, Mr. Gideon. I have committed no crime, I have nothing to hide. I live here with my family and I make a fair profit. That is all." After a pause, he added: "Yes, I shall be happy to have my lawyer present, if you please."

Gideon nodded, and then there came

footsteps outside and a tall, big-boned man whom he only vaguely recognised as Chief Inspector Archer came in, with Honiwell. Suddenly, something clicked in Gideon's mind: six or seven years ago this man had been a detective officer who had shown remarkable physical courage in a conflict with a criminal known as Micky the Slob. He had been gravely wounded, recovering after a long time. It was common these days for promotion to come quickly but Archer's had come very quickly indeed. He was a tall, rangy man, with clear grey eyes, and filled out since Gideon had known him.

"Good afternoon, sir. I'm sorry I was at the back when you arrived."

"No harm done," Gideon said. "Do you know Mr. Rataudi?"

"Yes, sir." Archer's face showed no expression.

"He has promised to come to Scotland Yard to answer some questions. Will you see that he has safe conduct?"

"I will, sir."

"Thanks," said Gideon, turning back to Rataudi.

It was quite impossible to guess what

was going on behind the brown eyes, the pupils prominent against the yellowish whites. The lashes were upswept, almost like a woman's. Rataudi had a honey-coloured skin, reminding Gideon of Juanita Concepcion, whom he had seen last night. Last night at the Ball seemed an age away! The Pakistani's face was so narrow, his nose and chin so long, it was almost as if in being born his features had been tightly compressed into a mould which had been shaped in this odd way. He had thin lips, too, very feminine in their curves and softness.

"Mr. Archer," Gideon said, still looking at Rataudi.

"Yes, sir?"

"Is there any report yet on how many died at Long Street?"

"Two bodies have been found so far," Archer replied. "One's a woman's."

Tension grew in the room. Rataudi moistened his lips, as if for the first time he began to realise the precariousness of his position; or possibly, to realise how dreadful were the consequences of his profiteering. But the expression soon faded and he looked quite blank.

Then Archer went on in an icy voice: "It appears that the cellar walls had been weakened by demolition to make room for sleeping bunks, Commander. Once the collapse started there was no support. *Every* wall had been weakened, and under pressure they just gave way."

Honiwell put in: "Killing people," quite laconically.

Rataudi drew a deep breath.

"I wish to make a statement," he declared. "I wish to state I am only one of three partners in this property development. I am not the one responsible for reconstructions and for expansion. There are others. Also," he added with a touch of dignity, "it was not possible to allow these people to stay out in the streets. I am proud to have helped to give so many of them shelter. Please understand. I am proud, not ashamed."

★　★　★

Gideon stepped into his office at half-past two that afternoon, vividly aware of what had happened. In one way it had been the most concentrated period of action he had known for years; in another, the period of the most agonising waiting.

There was still no news of Riddell.

He had driven from Lancelot Crescent to Long Street, past batteries of newspapermen and photographers, to find that the shifting of the rubble had been stopped because of damage to a gas main and the threat of fire. Every minute that Riddell or anyone else was buried there reduced the chance of finding them alive. There was still no certain count of the number of people buried, only that one more W.V.S. woman was missing as well as Riddell. All police, firemen and Civil Defence workers had been accounted for but there had been some volunteers as well as newspapermen and photographers, some of whom had been freelance; if anyone on the staff of a newspaper or television service was missing, reports would soon come through. Gideon had missed Hobbs on the way back to the Yard, but there would be word from him soon.

Gideon sat heavily at his desk, feeling nausea in his stomach and a heavy belt of pressure at the back of his head and over his eyes. He found it heavy going to dig into his mind for things which he needed to do, then suddenly thought: "Mrs. Riddell!" Immediately he put a call through to her home, but the operator said: "I've tried her for Mr. Hobbs, sir, but there's no reply."

"Keep trying every half-hour," urged Gideon, and replaced the receiver. He was surprised that Hobbs hadn't left a message about Riddell's wife, but who could be blamed for overlooking anything that day?"

He wished he felt better, then suddenly realised that he had only had coffee and a piece of toast for breakfast. He sent for a messenger, and an elderly man appeared, one who seemed to have been at the Yard forever.

"I've missed lunch, Joe," Gideon said.

"*That* won't do, sir. I'll get you something."

"Right away, please," Gideon urged.

The door closed behind the man's silvery hair, and Gideon stole a few moments to stand at the window. As always, the Thames and the view calmed him, reminding him that the life of London and the crime of London was still ebbing and flowing, that the two small areas where death and disaster had struck were oases in the vast desert of his metropolitan area.

"Desert!" he ejaculated. "Now I'm getting fanciful!" He pulled himself up and strode to the desk, made a note that Honiwell was to come at four o'clock, fully briefed over the Entwhistle case, and then pulled the new files towards him. There were three. He knew before he opened one that each was of importance; Hobbs wouldn't have troubled him with small and routine cases. "What else has been going on?" he asked aloud, making a note to call Scott-Marle as he opened the first folder.

At half-past eleven, while he had been on his way to Long Street, there had been a post office hold-up in the city; at least half a million poundworth of paper money and postal orders had been stolen. He felt a flush of relief that this was primarily a job for the City of London Police, but such crimes often overlapped. He put in a call to the Commissioner of the City Police, and was answered almost at once.

"Thanks for ringing," the City man said, "but I think we're all right, George.

What we do need is some help from the Thames Division; this loot might have been taken down the river. I've been in touch and the Thames is sending Singleton over. If you'd give formal authority for us to borrow him — "

"Of course," said Gideon, making a note.

"Thanks," said the City man, and could not have made it more clear that he was too preoccupied to talk much. " 'Bye. I — oh!" Feeling suddenly rang in his voice. "Quite a picnic you're having at Notting Hill!"

He rang off without another word.

"*Picnic*!" breathed Gideon.

He picked up the second file and ran through the contents slowly. It was a request, accompanied by a detailed report, for an investigation into the affairs of a prominent exporting and importing company dealing in watches, clocks and allied instruments, the board of which had reason to suspect its secretary of fraud within the firm itself, and also of fraud at Customs. If the board's suspicions were right, these crimes had been going on for several years and the total amount of loss involved was at least a million pounds. The last sentence of the covering letter read:

It is clearly possible that our suspicions are wrong, equally possible that if we allow those members of the staff under suspicion to be aware of our suspicions, attempts will be made to cover up any depredations, or conceivably to leave the country so as to escape the consequences of any criminal acts. For this reason we ask that the greatest discretion be used in getting in touch with us, and would be grateful if a responsible officer will make an appointment with the undersigned, at the private address given below.

Yours very truly,
Cyril Mayhew.

Beneath the clear signature the name was typed "Sir Cyril Mayhew", whose address was 214, Clavering Street, London, W.1. That was just behind Berkeley Square, Gideon knew: a street of gracious Georgian houses built by Nash. He put the report aside and immediately dialled Scott-Marle's office, thinking both as he moved and as he waited. It was only a few moments before Scott-Marle himself answered: he had an extension enabling either him or his secretary to answer.

"The Commissioner."

"Gideon, sir."

"Ah! I've been hoping to hear from you. Has Superintendent Riddell been found yet."

"I'm afraid not," Gideon answered.

He underwent a strange moment, a kind of metamorphosis; as if he were not himself but was a detached mind, looking at and marvelling at himself. For in those few minutes of studying the letter and report, Riddell had not been in his mind. All his thoughts, all his concentration, had been on the new case. He did not know whether his sudden awareness of this, his sense of shock at his own ability to shut out even a tragedy when coping with a new problem, revealed itself to Scott-Marle; he did know that Scott-Marle was waiting for him to go on.

"I will be advised the moment there is any news," he went on. "Meanwhile, I have Mr. Rataudi the landlord here for questioning."

"Unhurt?"

"Yes, sir. Possibly frightened, but I'm not sure yet," Gideon replied. "I'll go down and see him in half an hour or so. There should be a preliminary report from Saxby and his division by the time I've finished with Rataudi."

After a pause, Scott-Marle asked: "I'd like to know what there is to know at five o'clock. I've promised a report to the Under-Secretary at the Home Office by half-past five."

"Shall I come and see you?"

"Please. And keep me informed, meanwhile."

"I will, sir," Gideon promised formally. "Before you go — "

"Yes?"

"There's another thing," Gideon went on, and explained briefly about the letter from Sir Cyril Mayhew. There was no need to go into great detail, and when he was sure Scott-Marle had heard enough to grasp the situation, he went on: "It's a job for the Fraud Squad and also obviously for Customs, and it could become very delicate. Would you like me to handle it from here in the beginning, or work through Customs?"

There was a long pause, and then Scott-Marle replied drily:

"In this case you must double Commander and Assistant Commissioner, George! I shall leave it entirely to you."

And he rang off.

Gideon replaced his receiver slowly, smiling faintly yet feeling rueful. If that remark was a true indication, Scott-Marle was going to push very hard on the Assistant Commissionership issue. Was there any special reason for that? He turned the fraud case over in his mind as he opened the last file.

On top, clipped, was a note:

Riddell's wife doesn't answer the telephone. I've tried regularly. If there's no reply soon I'll send a man to see her.

Gideon smiled with satisfaction at Hobb's attitude, then settled down to read about the murder of a young woman named Rosamund Lee, during the night. Reading the report, a vivid one, about the way the girl had been suffocated, seeing a photograph of her as she lay dead and another, gay and bright-eyed as she had been only a few weeks ago, all thought of Riddell, the Notting Hill disaster and the fraud problem faded from his mind. He studied this report as if there was nothing else of importance to consider. And one of the things that came to his mind was that in this same part of Ealing, earlier last night, a young constable from *Uniform* had caught two theives red-handed, and that this had incidentally betrayed a man who had used an antique and secondhand shop to cover the buying and selling of stolen goods. They were not connected cases, of course, that would be too much of a coincidence. But was it possible that the men investigating the burglary and the stolen goods could have noticed anything which was even remotely related to the murder?

He must check with Division, to make sure.

CHAPTER 9

MEDLEY

POLICE Constable Percival Oswald had slept soundly that morning but on the first moment of waking he had been aware of the cyclist who had passed him while he had been on duty last night. So that must have been on his subconscious mind while he had slept. He had seen the cyclist just after three o'clock, for when on night duty, days became all topsy-turvy.

Oswald, who was a boarder in a private house not far from Ealing Common, was lucky in more ways than one. His landlady, an elderly but spritely widow, positively mothered him. He had only to bang on the floor with a stick which she placed by his bedside for that purpose, and she would be up with the tea and the newspapers. He had got in soon after eight in the morning and dropped off to sleep rightaway. Now it was nearly two o'clock by the watch at his bedside. He knocked, and sure enough, her footsteps soon sounded on the stairs; they met as he came out of the bathroom.

"Good morning, my hero!" she greeted him, beaming.

"What's all this?" he inquired. "I'm no hero."

"According to the *Evening Globe* you are," she declared.

There he was, in the reproduction of a photograph he had had taken soon after getting his uniform. This was next to a photograph of the antique shop and the backs of the two men he had caught. The detective sergeant who had appeared to belittle what he had done the previous night, had given him full credit. And for the first time he realised what a haul they had made.

One estimate puts the value of the stolen jewellery recovered at over thirty thousand pounds, said the *Evening Globe*. The police at Ealing are busy checking each item against the description of stolen jewellery. A great number of people who lost valued heirlooms and jewels of great sentimental value may soon be overjoyed.

"And I've turned away *four* reporters," his landlady reported, with both pride and satisfaction. "It's amazing how they find out where you live, isn't it? Oh, there's a note for you from the station, a policeman brought it round and said you had to have it by two o'clock." It was characteristic of her to turn away at once, saying: "I'll have bacon and eggs for you in half an hour — that's at a quarter to three *sharp*, mind!"

She closed the door on her own trim figure, in a plain grey dress which matched her thick, grey hair, neatly groomed as if she had a secret hope of being photographed with her hero.

Oswald opened the letter, which was from the Divisional Superintendent. The gist was that he should report at four o'clock at the Headquarters, and if questioned by any newspapermen "or any other person" he was to say nothing. He read through the newspaper story on him again, and went to bathe and shave. He was delighted with his recognition, deeply satisfied that he had passed his first real test so well, yet nagged by the memory of the man on the bicycle. There had been something about the way the man had averted his face, had pedalled so stiffly, almost as if he had a guilty conscience. He heard a ring at the front door bell and suspected another newspaperman, but Mrs. Stilwell let this caller in, and a woman's voice sounded.

The woman was still talking, over sizzling bacon and spluttering eggs, when he went downstairs; the little dining room was off the old-fashioned kitchen. Mrs. Stilwell came out with a laden plate, and there was toast, butter and marmalade already on the table. He sensed something in the air as the caller, a near neighbour, looked over Mrs. Stilwell's shoulder. Of course, it might simply be that she had come to welcome the "hero". Oswald, who had a natural humility, was already laughing at himself.

"Well," the neighbour said. "Go on, tell him."

"Elsie, *do* let him have his breakfast first."

"You tell him or I shall," declared Elsie. "It isn't often you have a chance to tell a *copper* anything about crime."

Oswald's heart missed a beat. It was now apparent that she hadn't come about his previous night's success. There was something else. Elsie was a short, very tubby woman in her early thirties, with plain features and a spotty skin but quite dazzlingly pale, honey-brown eyes and beautiful, silky golden hair. Her lips were red and very moist and whenever he saw her he thought her one of the most sensuous women he had ever met; or was voluptuous the word?

"What's been going on?" he inquired, slicing into an egg so that the bright yellow yolk oozed out over one of the three crisp rashers of bacon.

Elsie breathed: "*Murder!*"

Mrs. Stilwell said in a choky voice: "There's been a murder, in *Ealing*."

"On our doorstep," Elsie gasped.

"Near where you were last night," Mrs. Stilwell told him. "In Caerphilly Street."

He thought: Caerphilly Street, off Cardiff Road. For a moment he felt almost too choked to eat, but he knew he must not show too much excitement, so he put bacon and egg into his mouth, ate, and then said:

"You've been dreaming."

"Oh, no, I haven't," Elsie insisted, her

eyes becoming even brighter. "It was on the radio at half-past one, don't you make any mistake about *that*. It said a girl had been suffocated with her own pillow. You can't even be safe in your own bed at night! They didn't find her until someone came round from her office, she worked at Hammersmith, to see why she hadn't turned up, and when there was no answer the landlord opened her door. It's a house of bed-sitter flatlets you see, like mine, and they found her, absolutely dead she was, been dead for *hours* . . ."

Oswald did not interrupt, nor did he take everything in, except the fact that the woman had been murdered about the time he had caught the two men at the shop.

* * *

Rosamund Lee's lovely body, stiff now with *rigor mortis*, was on a mortuary slab, and would soon be under the *post mortem* examination.

In the north of England her mother and father had been told of her death, and the mother was in a state of shock.

In the heart of London, only a few

buildings away from Mayhew & Company, Importers and Exporters, David Wells was at his desk. Most of the time he was able to concentrate on the figures and the analyses on which he was working, but every now and again a strange chill took possession of him and the figures and the letters blurred. Whenever this happened he gripped his pen tightly and raised his head and stared at the plain calender pinned to the wall in front of his desk. After a while, he began to realise what caused these spasms, in which he could *see* Rosamund in his mind's eye, could almost *feel* her closeness.

There was a girl, Lucy Chalmers, at a desk behind him, typing most of the time. But occasionally someone would move across and speak to her, and when she spoke she sounded like Rosamund.

It was getting worse.

Clenching his fists did not drive the chill away any more. Instead, it seemed to send it coursing through his whole body. And it took longer to get back to the job again, was much more difficult to concentrate. But he had to, because there was so much to do, and also because there were dozens of others in the office who would notice if he behaved oddly.

He did not know that Lucy Chalmers was watching him all the time, wondering what was worrying him.

At his home, in Chiswick, not very far from Ealing, his wife Ellen was baking scones, which he liked, and preparing a Lancashire hot pot, which he liked, and wondering which book he would like from the library, just round the corner. All of these things occupied her mind a little, but what most preoccupied her was how to keep the children quiet when he came home. She had become more and more aware that they got on his nerves with their shouting and squabbling; he hadn't anything like the patience with them that he'd shown a year ago, although they had been just as noisy, then.

Behind all this preoccupation was another: their own relationship, David's and hers.

She had known years ago that he had *affaires*; but then he had had *affaires* before they were married, she had been one of them! She never knew why he had married her, but for several years she had been contented, if never excited, and had always been able to tell when he had been out with another woman: he invariably brought her flowers or chocolates! Or, before the days when baby-sitters were needed, he had taken her to the theatre or the pictures. And all the time he had been gay with her, and ready to help with household chores.

Two years ago, soon after the birth of their third child, he had begun to change. Everything he did with her was an effort. Often, he would be short-tempered. She was beginning to lose him, and tried desperately to find a way to keep him at least to hold the house together.

What would she do, if he left her?

Apart from the agony it would mean to her, how could she manage with the children?

He had been out last night, she knew, but he had come home eventually; the awful thing would be if, one day, he simply did not return to her.

*　*　*

On the other side of London, in Tottenham, another woman was thinking about her problems, which could hardly have been more different. She was Netta Jameson, wife of an alcoholic with whom she had not lived for ten years and from whom she had not received a penny in those years. She had once been so desperately in love with him and had lived through the anguish of a dying love: first his, then hers. It had not seriously occurred to her that she would ever fall in love again, and if she had a deep regret it was that she had never had a child. For the past ten years she had first managed and then become part-owner of a small but exclusive fur *salon* in Tottenham, from which she earned a comfortable three thousand pounds a year, after paying tax. She was never at a loss for an escort but only very seldom took a lover, then invariably out of a kind of compassion, not out of any deep, emotional feeling.

One day, over a year ago, the *salon* had been burgled, and nearly everything of value had been taken. Although fully covered by insurance, the raid had made her very angry indeed.

The local police had not soothed her, although they had used platitude after platitude. There were a lot of fur robberies, it was never possible to be sure whether the stock would be recovered. Had she taken the right precautions? There had even seemed a hint that she was partly to blame for not installing the most expensive and up-to-date burglar alarm. She had not hesitated to show her anger, demanded to see a senior officer from Scotland Yard. It had not occurred to her that the police would ever send such a man.

To this day, she could remember when Matt Honiwell had first appeared.

She had been alone in the shop, her partner and an assistant being out having coffee, when he had come in. It had not occurred to her that he was a policeman, he looked so — well, not untidy, not ruffled or rumpled, just not official-looking. An uncle of a man. He had closed the door carefully behind him, smiled — and, as she advanced towards him — seemed to freeze.

And, in a way, she had gone still and cold, too.

He said afterwards that it had not been simply because she was the most attractive woman he had ever seen, but that something seemed to have exploded within him. He had been warned to expect a shrew, and found instead a Venus. He had been dumbstruck. At last, he had thawed, and soon astonished her by introducing himself as Chief Superintendent Honiwell of the C.I.D.

"You *are* a Scotland Yard man?" she had exclaimed.

"I know I don't look the part, and that fools a lot of people," he had replied in a pleasant voice, not too deep. He had good features, although then, as now, he had been a little too fat. Well, plump. "There has been a series of burglaries from fur *salons* lately," he had gone on to say, "and all of them have been from shops fitted with the same make of burglar alarms. May I see yours?"

It had been one of the make he had been looking for.

On it, he had found the smear of a fingerprint.

From this print he had been able to make some arrests, and had recovered most of the goods stolen from her stock. On the day when he had come to tell her so, he had asked, to her great surprise:

133

"Will you have dinner with me tonight, to celebrate?"

And, accepting, she had been surprised by her own eagerness.

Within two months they had set up house together, with some misgivings but none of them on moral grounds. He was a widower looked after by his married daughter; Netta was married to an alcoholic, who refused to divorce her. Until meeting Matt Honiwell she had not particularly cared whether she was free or not. Once he had discovered that she was with a man, her husband had reiterated with malice if not malevolence that he would never give her a divorce.

"Let them live in sin," he had sneered when with mutual friends or relatives, and no one could shift his resolve.

They were happy, growing contented: as the ecstasies of their early days became less frequent, their companionship and pride in each other became much greater. After the first few months, however, Netta had been sure that something about their relationship troubled Matt, but it was not until after the Ball the previous night that he had told her what.

"Almost certainly nothing to worry about," he had said, "but I'd feel happier from the Yard's point of view if we were married." He had shot her an amused sideways glance as he drove. "Do you remember that craggy-looking man, Singleton, from the Thames Division?"

"Yes," she had said.

"He reminded me of one of our men whose wife left him and lived with another man. He was so jealous that he went on the hard liquor and drank himself so silly that he attempted to murder his wife. The charge was reduced and he was sentenced to three years' imprisonment for attempting to cause grievous bodily harm; he's due out of prison in a few weeks' time."

"I remember reading about the case," she said. "But darling, I can't see you losing your head and going to Rupert with the intention of killing him."

"No," he had said, "nor can I. It — oh, well, I'd much rather marry you than not!"

They had left it there, but she wondered several times whether there had been anything else in his mind. She would have to ask him, soon. If it *did* prey on him then it might spoil his pride in and efficiency at police work, the last thing he must allow to happen.

A customer came in, and she pushed the reverie to the back of her mind.

*　*　*

In another part of London, the three children of the convicted Entwhistle who was under sentence of life imprisonment for the murder of their mother, all played together: the elder children, Clive now thirteen and Jennifer now eleven, quite happily. But the youngest daughter, Carol, not quite ten, went up to the room she shared with her sister. She often appeared to prefer to be on her own, a quiet and secretive child. Although she had been too young at the time of the murder to know the full implications, both then and now she seemed more affected than the others by the fact that her father was in prison. This afternoon, she went to a shelf of books beside her bed, pulled out several, and then took one which was lodged at the back, out of sight unless the shelves were thoroughly dusted, a task which her aunt left to her.

This was a beautifully illustrated book on the county of Devon.

There were the coves and inlets, the rocks and the sea; there were the small towns and the villages, the forests and trees. She opened the book immediately to a page near the end, a natural opening, because inside was a photograph of her mother and father, taken just before he had left for Africa. She could remember, tiny though she had been, that her father had hoisted her high, laughed, and promised:

"I'm going to build a bridge across a big river, and when it's done I'll be back to carry you across it."

He had come back, her mother had been killed, and he had been taken away by the police, and put on trial at a place called the Old Bailey, somewhere in London, and soon afterwards sent to Dartmoor — to the prison.

There it was, grey and ugly and forbidding, with tiny barred windows and huge spike-topped walls, set amid the bright green of the pasture with a background of trees clad in the soft light green of spring.

He was there.

He wrote to them regularly, on buff-coloured paper, often by hand, sometimes on a typewriter. Whenever it was by hand, he wrote at the top: *"The Library"*. Perhaps they both realised that their closest contact was through books.

She studied every window, every bar, every wall and every door, wondering where exactly her father was . . .

At that moment he was in the library at the prison, writing; not to her but to one of the prison visitors, with his never-ending plea for help in getting a retrial. There was one sentence which appeared in every letter he wrote (except to the children). *"I did not kill my wife"*. He was sitting at a bare table, writing a sentence at a time, and looking up every now and again as if seeking words from the books on the shelves and the newspapers and magazines neat in their racks. A warder in the library kept glancing at him covertly; at the sunken cheeks and the sunken but fever-bright eyes. Although he worked outside a great deal, his skin was like wax and there seemed no health in him.

He was tormented, and the years brought

no solace — only greater torment, greater bitterness, burning hatred for the man who had killed his wife and allowed him to pay the penalty of guilt.

MURDERER

THE man who had murdered Entwhistle's wife was in his office, a tiny
one with a window which overlooked
the Thames just below Tower Bridge and a
corner of Billingsgate Market. On hot days,
when he opened the window, a strong
odour of fish would sweep in, and he never
really became used to it. Yet if one could
forget the stench there was such beauty on
the river, with its changing colours and
changing surface, the pale blue and dark
blue, the nearby green; the silvery mirror-
calmness, gold-tinted with the morning
and evening sun; the rippling by the wind
or by passing barges, small tugs, pleasure
boats or police launches; the rough, when
the wind blew furiously; or the pocked,
when heavy rain fell straight down like
bullets.

He sat at a desk pushed against the wall
beneath the window, so that whenever he
looked up he had a panoramic view. From
the tiny office behind him his secretary

typed with a compulsive vigour. She was nearing fifty but seemed neither younger nor older than when she had first worked for him when he had become manager of the department, which dealt mostly in carpets, tapestries, silks and cottons from India and the Far East. She was plump, and squeezed her breasts too tightly into a brassière which was larger than most. She had a tightly confined waist and spreading hips. Her hair was cut all round her head at a level with her only attractive feature, little pink ears, and she had taken to wearing angel's wing glasses with a frame of mother of pearl. Perhaps to compensate for her physical drawbacks, she was almost incredibly swift and efficient, doing the work of at least two able secretaries and, having been in this department for over thirty years, she had accumulated knowledge and experience which increased her value tenfold. Her name was Bessie Smith.

Greenwood was very thoughtful that afternoon, and Bessie was aware of it. Every few months, her employer had an *affaire*. The girl or woman concerned never came to the office, and always telephoned the private number which Greenwood had on his desk. All three department managers had one, for that matter: Greenwood, the manager who dealt mostly in spices, teas, cocoa and other foodstuffs, and the third who looked after the precious and semi-precious stones of the East, including ivory and porcelain. All three of them, when on buying trips abroad, also bought basket and wickerwork, wood carvings and a great variety of curios at prices so absurdly low that at times they seemed to make more profit out of these trifles than the more expensive products, such as jewellery and carpets and silks.

The original partners in the firm, Cox and Shieling Limited, were still active in the business although they did not travel much; they concentrated on their extensive holdings in London property. The firm was one of the most widely known in the Far East, much more familiar in Hong Kong, Tokyo, Singapore and Bangkok, for instance, than it was in London.

Bessie Smith glanced up as the door leading from his office opened. The silence from the clattering typewriter seemed profound.

"Bessie," he said, "I think it's time I checked the carpet factories in Mirzapore and Bangalore; I haven't been too pleased with the quality of the carpets we've been getting lately."

Ah, ha! thought Bessie, he's breaking it off again.

"Shall I check the flights, Mr. Greenwood?"

"Flights and ships," he said. "I might combine the trip with a holiday. It's ages since I had more than a few days off."

"Yes, Mr. Greenwood," said Bessie. "I'll have some flights and sailings by this time tomorrow."

"Thanks." He nodded as he looked at the thick pile of letters by her typewriter. He did not marvel that she had done so much, simply took her prodigious capacity for work for granted. "Is the draft contract ready for Lin Goh of Singapore?"

Even for her that was half a day's work, and he hadn't given her his pencilled rough until mid-morning.

"No," she said. "But I'll have it by tomorrow."

He nodded, without say another word,

picked up the pile of letters and drafts and took them into his own office for signing. She did not start typing again immediately, but stared at the closed door. He was a nice-looking man, five feet ten or so, lean, always well dressed, perhaps a little too well-groomed, but none of these things concerned Bessie, who had long since come to terms with her personal and sex life. Much more important, Eric Greenwood was very good at his job, and no one bought at a sharper price. But these days he didn't keep his mind on his job as much as he should. The older he got, the shorter his *affaires* seemed to become.

Aloud, she said: "I wonder who the poor little bitch is this time," and then began to pound afresh on her typewriter.

Over the years, she had acquired quite a remarkable facility to type accurately and even think intelligently about her job, and also to day-dream in a special sort of way. She weaved romances, seldom physical, about men she met at the pub where she had a counter snack every day and a Guinness every evening after work. She knew they were ridiculous but nevertheless enjoyed the fantasies.

Just now, she typed and dreamed of Sam Benbow.

He had come to work at Billingsgate, he said, and by gee he smelt like it! He was easy to talk to, a sympathetic listener, and very interested in her job and what she could tell him of the oriental places Cox and Shieling brought their goods from. She didn't quite remember when he had started talking about sheiks and harems and Muslims and their four wives or however many it was. Nor did she remember when she had retorted that a lot of Englishmen had as much you-know-what as any old sheik, with none of the responsibilities. Certainly she had not the faintest idea how much, at odd times and in odd phrases, she had told Sam about Eric Greenwood and his mistresses.

But Detective Sergeant Benbow of the C.I.D. had it all carefully recorded and precisely phrased in a report now ready for Chief Detective Superintendent Honiwell.

Eric Greenwood's latest *affaire* was with a pretty and vivacious young woman, who he knew was going to cause him trouble. Some of his mistresses were venomous and vicious when he broke off, some were tearful and pleading; now and again one accepted the congé without any outward show of emotion. Usually, he chose married women, preferably those losing their freshness. He found more sexual satisfaction and excitement with them than with an inexperienced and possibly timid girl, and when he tired of their looks he simply dropped them. He always began when their husbands were away for some months (as with Entwhistle's wife, three years ago), because no matter what their feelings, few actually wanted to break their marriage. Greenwood had long since come to regard the difficulties and unpleasantnesses of breaking off an *affaire* as the price, virtually the only price, he had to pay for his pleasures. From the beginning he had always been extremely careful, making sure no one visited him at work, having early rendezvous at small hotels before taking his lights o'love to his small, anonymous bachelor flat in Camberwell — and never the same hotel twice. There were problems in this, of course, but he prepared his conquests with great precision and often enjoyed the actual planning as much as the conquest itself.

Only once before this, had he been faced with any problem. Margaret Entwhistle had wanted to tell her husband, get a divorce and marry him, Eric.

He had killed her . . .

For a while, just a few short hours, he had felt a terrible sense of guilt and remorse; he had actually gone to St. Ludd's Cathedral in silent confession, in a kind of plea for forgiveness. That had coincided with an attempt to steal some of the plate from the altar, a sacrilege he had been able to prevent.

So, he had considered himself forgiven in the eyes of the Lord.

What he did not know was that he was a schizophrenic, that he could commit a crime, do evil, and then put it out of his mind, feeling no sense of guilt. It was not that he thought himself right to kill, only that he was right to save himself. It was not that he could not tell right from wrong; it was that when the wrong had been committed he virtually forgot it.

As he had "forgotten" murdering Margaret Entwhistle.

As he had "forgotten" allowing her husband to stand trial, and be sentenced to imprisonment for life for his, Greenwood's, crime.

Now, he was remembering . . .

For Jennifer Goodenough, whom he had known for only three months, was proving very difficult indeed.

She was younger than some of his mistresses, in her early thirties, and very attractive in her blonde way. There was no doubt at all that she intended to maintain the association although her husband was due home, in a very few days, from a three months' voyage on a merchant vessel; due to bring to London a cargo of carpets, tapestries, silks and cottons for the West End salerooms of Cox and Shieling. That was how Greenwood and Jennifer had met: he had gone with some last minute bills of lading for European goods being supplied to the Orient, and Jennifer had been there to see her husband off for his long voyage. When the ship, the *Orianda*, registered at London, had cast off and while her husband was still waving to her, Greenwood had said:

"Will you come and have some lunch..."

She was a remarkable woman; that night, they had shared his bed.

She had not shown her clinging propensity at first, but only when the *Orianda* had left the West African port of Dakar, its last port of call on the homeward run. He had begun his usual "I hate it but we must part" gambit, and she had simply laughed it off.

"No, darling, this arrangement suits me very well," she had retorted. "A husband at sea and a lover at home. And *you* shouldn't grumble, he's always away a lot more than he's at home."

Greenwood had realised his folly then; she knew where he worked, could come and visit him, did in fact telephone him but, thank God, on his personal line. She could make a great deal of trouble with the company, which was small enough for scandal to be ruinous. And the *Orianda* was one of several cargo vessels owned by the company through an associate firm. Once he had realised all the implications and the danger, he had tried to force the issue.

"It's one thing to have a passionate *affaire* for a few weeks, sweetheart, another to be permanently attached. You should realise that I don't like permanent arrangements. If I did I'd have been married years ago."

"*Darling*," she had said only this morning, "we are permanent. If you care to go off and have your peccadilloes when Simon's home I won't complain, but when he's gone *we* are together. Or Cox and Shieling might be very disappointed with one of their managers."

"Jennifer," he had said, "don't threaten me."

"Eric," she had retorted, "if Cox and Shieling knew that their trusted manager for carpets and fabrics had stolen the wife of their trusted first mate on the good ship *Orianda*, do you think they would stand for it?"

The truth was, he couldn't be sure; in fact, he didn't think they would.

And the truth was, he was frightened of both Jennifer and Simon Goodenough.

And the truth was, she was caging him; was far too possessive; in the past two months she had acted much more like a demanding wife than an acquiescent mistress. He *must* free himself from her, but he did not think she would give him that freedom easily.

Margaret Entwhistle had threatened it, too.

Greenwood finished signing the letters and left them on his desk, went out a little after five o'clock with a casual "Goodnight" to Bessie, and walked down the rickety wooden stairs, then along the cobbled lane which led to Cannon Street and his bus. He bought a newspaper from his usual news-stand, within the shadow of the three-fold steeple of St. James, Gardickhythe, and close to the now closed and shuttered doors of Billingsgate Market. As he unfolded the newspaper he glanced fondly at the fifteenth-century stone church, which he had helped to protect once from Nazi fire-bombs and once from a fanatic's sabotage; then he looked at the headlines.

GIRL SUFFOCATED

London Hunt for Killer

He read the story with deepening interest as he walked along to his bus stop and on the bus. Unbidden thoughts crowded his mind. There was a murderer at large. The victim lived in Ealing. Jennifer lived in

Acton, which was very close by. Murders often ran in pairs, in series. Already this newspaper was talking about the possibility of the killer being psychopathic. If there were another, similar murder soon, there would be much more talk of a psychopathic killer, it ought to work out very well.

After all, it had, once.

He had a week in which to plan.

* * *

That was the very moment when the Yard's telephone rang on Gideon's desk, and as he lifted it a man cried with excitement, even joy.

"Riddell's been pulled out, George. He's alive!"

* * *

That had been the best moment of the day for Gideon.

The day had been as topsy-turvy as any he had known, and even the ever-reliable Honiwell had called to ask to postpone the meeting about Entwhistle until the next day.

"The man Benbow, who's doing a very good job on the case, is hopeful of results tonight," Honiwell had said. "So if it's all right with you, Commander, I'll come in the morning."

"Come round to my place tonight and we'll eat and talk," Gideon said. "I may be up to my eyes in the immigrant business in the morning. Say nine o'clock."

Honiwell said: "I'll be there."

As a result Gideon had been able to give more time and thought to the Ealing murder, had a private report on his desk about P.C. Oswald as well as cuttings from all the newspapers; he hoped these would not go to the young officer's head. He had thought more about the request from Mayhew: obviously the Yard or the City Police or both should plant a man in the firm which was probably the victim of serious embezzlement. As obviously he would have to see Mayhew, and whenever he thought of that he was ruefully aware of the "threat" of the Assistant Commissionership.

How many men in his position would dream of calling it a threat?

All the afternoon there had been the anxiety about Riddell; now the blessed relief that he was alive made everything else seem of little importance.

CHAPTER 11

DESPAIR AND JOY

ACCORDING to the rescue workers, it was a miracle that Riddell had not died. He had been protected by a beam in the wall which had broken and made a kind of arch under which he had been trapped. He was badly cut and bruised and there were fractured ribs and the danger of severe injury both to his head and his pelvis, but he was not only alive, he actually came round after he had been placed in the ambulance.

Gideon received this report from Saxby, who sounded exhausted, but Gideon forebore to advise him to stop work for the day.

"I keep thinking, shouldn't we let Riddell's wife know?" Saxby suggested.

"That's being looked after."

"I should have known," Saxby said in a lighter tone, but soon he was sounding troubled and over-glum again. One of the W.V.S. women and a freelance reporter were dead and seven people, all Pakistanis, six of them women, were in hospital in a serious condition. Over twenty others had received treatment at the same hospital. "None of the Fire Service, Civil Defence or our chaps were hurt, except Riddell," went on Saxby. And then added abruptly: "Commander, I'm as worried as hell. May I come and talk to you?"

Obviously, he felt in great need to unburden himself, and it would be cruel as well as possibly damaging to say no.

"Come right away," he invited, more glad than ever that Honiwell had postponed his visit.

"Give me about half an hour," begged Saxby, and rang off.

Gideon picked up his direct line telephone and dialled his own home number; as the *brrr-brrr-brrr* sounded, the Yard's exchange bell rang. He picked the receiver up and put it to his other ear, saying:

"Gideon."

"Commander, Mrs. Riddell is on the telephone, I've got her at last."

"Ah," said Gideon. "Put her through." At the same time Kate answered on the other telephone, and he covered the exchange mouthpiece with his hand and said quietly: "Kate, love, I'll be at least an hour late. Don't wait dinner for me."

"George," she began, "is Tom — "

"Out and alive," Gideon told her. "I've Mrs. Riddell on the line now. Bye." He put the one receiver down and spoke into the other mouthpiece in much the same tone of voice, suddenly and embarrassedly aware that he didn't know Mrs. Riddell's first name. "Mrs. Riddell," he said. "I've both bad and good news for you, about Tom."

He didn't know whether she had heard anything over the radio or seen anything of the Long Street disaster on television. He saw a mental picture of her at the Ball, with her feathered dress and feathered cap and wrinkled face and little pinched beak of a nose and point of a chin.

"Please tell me the good first," she pleaded in her high-pitched voice.

What *was* her Christian name. It was on the tip of his tongue but wouldn't come.

"He's been dug out from a pile of rubble which collapsed on top of him, he's alive, and he's on his way to St. Mary's Hospital, Paddington, if he isn't there already. He'll receive immediate examination, not a minute will be lost, and as far as I've yet been told there's no serious injury."

He stopped, and in that second, he remembered: her name was Violet, called Vi. She seemed to be breathing very evenly; hissingly, as if she had some slight obstruction in her nostrils.

Quietly, she asked: "Will it help if I go straight to the hospital?"

"I doubt it," Gideon said. "It would be better if you could stay near your telephone, Vi, or near one with friends," he added hastily.

"I would rather stay here, Mr. Gideon," she replied in the same high-pitched but calm voice. "I'm sure I can rely on you to let me know if there is any more news."

"You can rely on that absolutely," Gideon promised.

"Thank you," replied Riddell's wife. "You are very kind."

When she rang off, Gideon had a suspicion that she had a sob in her voice, but he could not be certain. He was sure that someone ought to go and see whether she needed help, but was far from knowing who would be best. He was deliberating when two things happened at once: the door from Hobbs's room opened on a tap, and Hobbs looked in, and the direct line telephone on his desk rang. Very few people knew that number, he used it almost exclusively for outgoing calls he did not want overheard. He motioned Hobbs in, and said gruffly: "Gideon."

"George," Kate said. "I'd like to go and see Violet Riddell. Can you give me her address?"

Gideon hesitated only for a moment before saying: "Yes, Kate, I can. She lives at Wembley — " He looked up at Hobbs, standing by the desk and Hobbs formed "Riddell?" with his lips. Gideon nodded and Hobbs went on clearly as Gideon held the telephone out to him: "14, one-four, Anderson Drive, repeat *Anderson* Drive, Wembley. I believe it's near the Stadium."

"Did you get that?" Gideon asked, drawing the telephone close.

"Yes," Kate said. "If I'm not back when you get home, Penny will have something ready for supper." She paused before going on with a tremor in her voice: "Be careful, George."

"*I'm* all right." He tried to sound bluff. "See you later, love."

He rang off, and waved to a chair. Hobbs sat down and leaned back, crossing his legs at the ankles. He was so poised and confident, and there was something in his manner which Gideon had always found hard to identify. Perhaps it was inborn authority. And although he wasn't a dandy, he was always so well-dressed: just enough white cuff showing at each wrist, his collar invariably looking as if he had just put it on. Gideon did not speak although the period of silent reflection was long drawn-out. Then he took a large-bowled pipe from his left-hand pocket and smoothed the shiny wood; he seldom smoked this (or anything else) these days, but fondled it at periods of tension or emotional stress, especially when the day had been hard. He laid this pipe on the desk and opened a cupboard in the desk, taking out a bottle of Scotch whisky and some glasses and bottles of soda water.

"Alec?"

"Just a finger, and fill the glass up, will you?"

Gideon mixed two drinks of about the same strength, handed one to Hobbs and raised his own.

"Cheers."

"Cheers."

"Quite a day."

"Which could have turned out to be a lot worse," Hobbs remarked.

"Yes." Gideon sipped again. "We make quite a team."

Hobbs seemed to stiffen, very slightly.

"You and me?"

"Yes."

"*Quite* a team," Hobbs agreed, and put his glass to his lips. "Here's to its future."

They drank, while many thoughts passed through Gideon's mind, the most vivid perhaps that Hobbs was in love with his, Gideon's, Penny. How *were* they getting on? Had their happiness at the Ball been an indication? What did Penny really think as she stormed, as it were, through boy-friend after boyfriend, always returning to Alec? "Uncle" Alec? No, there was some-thing more in her feelings for Hobbs than that. This could be the moment to ask, but something warned him not to. So he said:

"Saxby's coming over."

"I think I can guess why," Hobbs said. "Archer, his second-in command, is very good, very alert, very much on the ball. He told me a little. Saxby is afraid he himself has slipped up badly. He is inclined to blame himself for what happened at Long Street."

Gideon pursed his lips.

"Based on the reasoning that if he'd done more, or taken action earlier, or even reported to me, this disaster need never have happened?"

"Yes," Hobbs replied.

"That makes two of us," Gideon remarked, heavily.

"I thought you might feel like that, George," Hobbs said. "I long since gave up trying to convince you that you shouldn't try to carry all London's crime on your shoulders. The responsibility at Notting Hill isn't and never has been basically ours. It's a local authority and Ministry of Housing task, as well as one for the Home Office. You didn't neglect it. Nor did I. Nor did Riddell."

"I could have done a damned sight more than I did," Gideon growled, but he sat back, took another sip, and put his pipe away. "Do you know anything more about what's worrying Saxby?"

"Yes," answered Hobbs. "He thinks that there will be a lot of trouble after what happened today. He's only just faced the fact that there is a potentially violent group of Pakistani and Jamaican youths who have sunk their differences and formed a version of Black Power between them. One or two white youths have joined them. So far its activities have veen very limited, but he is sure they started the attack on Rataudi's house and would have lynched him had they got there in time."

Gideon thrust his lower jaw forward, looking startlingly Churchillian.

"How is it they didn't?"

"Archer placed a guard outside the house in Lancelot Crescent the moment he heard of the Long Street trouble, so we were one step ahead all the time," Hobbs exclaimed simply. "When we did have a job to do, George, we really did it. We really do have a good team!"

Gideon relaxed enough to smile, if grimly.

"Soft soap," he said. "But good. I like the sound of Archer."

"He hero-worships you," Hobbs stated.

"Oh, nonsense!" Gideon waved both hands, never knowing what to say when anyone made such a remark to him, and the more affected because this was from Hobbs. Of course, Hobbs was trying to dispel that feeling of responsibility, almost of guilt, that he knew Gideon felt; nevertheless, Hobbs very seldom used extravagant phrases and always said precisely what he meant in the most dispassionate way possible. "I doubt if he knows me except as a figurehead."

Hobbs laughed.

"David Archer," he said. "Micky the Slob."

At that instant Gideon had an even more vivid flashback to the case that must be ten — yes, at least ten — years old. A deadly man; a threat to blow-up a cargo vessel in London's docks; a good-looking young detective officer, public school, exceptional physical courage and a man full of ideas and, even when dealing with the Commander, not afraid to put those ideas forward. Just after the Micky the Slob arrest, Archer had been savagely attacked and left for dead.

Now that he recalled so much in detail, Gideon also recalled seeing Archer's name on the promotion list; but he did not remember seeing him promoted to Chief

Inspector at Notting Hill. It could have happened when he had been on leave, for Hobbs now took over a lot of routine jobs. All the same he, Gideon, ought to keep in touch.

"He hasn't forgotten a thing about you," Hobbs declared. "He even went so far as to say that you were the deciding factor in his staying in the Force when he recovered from the knifing." Hobbs paused, and then went on: "He didn't put this into words but the picture as I see it is that he's been pushing Saxby to take more notice of the Black Power fire-brands and Saxby has taken the view that they're just teenage hotheads. Now Saxby has changed his mind."

As Hobbs talked, Gideon felt a growing sense of alarm — of depression also because of the obvious failures — but mostly of alarm. For there had been hatred in many of the youths at Lancelot Crescent, and when the full extent of the Long Street disaster was known, that hatred might become much fiercer. The racial problems in Britain, especially in London, had caused a great deal of simmering resentments but apart from occasional conflicts between individuals and small groups it had never really erupted. If ever it did, if ever that simmering sense of bitterness and injustice felt by so many immigrants flared up, and at the same time the anti-immigration elements burst its bonds, then one of the ugliest situations imaginable would be created.

Hatred, race hatred, would be let loose in violence.

Of course, this had always been his fear, the underlying reason for his disquiet. That was why he found it so inevitable that he should shoulder some of the blame. What he had to deal with now, however, was an impending situation which could lead to disaster. It was a matter of extreme urgency.

He knew that Hobbs had some idea of what was passing through his mind: they worked together so much that often very little needed saying. He was very anxious to see Saxby, and was more than ever anxious to put the right man on to the investigation into the Black Power group.

"Can Archer work with Rollo?" he asked.

"I should think they would make a good pair."

"What about Piluski?"

Hobbs considered, and then asked: "Why?"

"He faced the same kind of situation as the immigrants much of his life."

"Being Jewish, you mean?" Hobbs finished his drink and put the glass on a sheet of paper on Gideon's desk; he placed his hands on the arms of his chair, as if he was about to spring to his feet. But he sat still, staring at Gideon. A long silence followed, and Gideon knew that Hobbs was fighting a kind of battle within himself.

Gideon's Scotland Yard exchange telephone bell rang. He put out a hand, lifted the receiver, said: "Whoever it is, have them hold on or call me later," and put the receiver down. Hobbs was still gripping the arms of his chair. He must be on the sharp edge of real dilemma or he would not ponder this so long.

At last, he said: "Piluski has the right temperament. He could move among all sides and win a hearing, probably win a lot of confidence. But would he be up to this emotionally, George? Would it hurt him too much to work among the people who are victims of this situation? Would he feel too bitter to be detached?" When Gideon didn't answer, Hobbs went on as if desperately anxious to make himself absolutely clear. "Would he be pro-immigrant to begin with, just as Riddell was pro-white or at least anti-colour?"

Gideon reflected only for a few moments before saying: "I don't think so, but you might be right. We'll put Rollo on to the job at once and talk to Piluski when we've thought about him more." As Hobbs nodded, his tension easing, he picked up the receiver and demanded: "Who wanted me?"

He half-expected it to be Saxby, or Honiwell, who must have felt there was no end to waiting.

"It's Mr. Wilson, of Ealing," the operator said. "Just one moment, sir."

In the ensuing pause Gideon had time to remember that he had meant to call about the Ealing murder, had meant to find out whether the men at the antique shop had noticed anything which might possibly help with the investigation into the murder which had taken place nearby. Not having time to call Wilson was not one of those things he could blame himself for. He

pushed the murder file over to Hobbs, said:
"This is Gideon," and then heard the
Ealing man say:

"Commander?"

"Yes, Jack. How are you?"

"I think this is one of my weeks,"
answered Wilson, satisfaction resonant in
his voice. "The total amount of stolen
jewellery recovered is over sixty thousand
pounds, and we've identified a quarter of it
as from burglaries in or near *this* Division."
Small wonder Wilson sounded cock-a-
hoop. "But that isn't the only problem we
have, you know; there's that poor kid's
murder. And we *might* have had a break
over that." He could not keep the excitement out of his voice.

Even Gideon's heart leapt.

"How big a break?"

"I've just talked to the constable —
Oswald — who caught the two burglars.
He saw a man cycling from the direction of
Caerphilly Road at about three o'clock this
morning," Wilson reported. "He got a fair
look at the chap but didn't see his face too
clearly — there was only the street light,
and Oswald had a fit of sneezing. But
Oswald's sure he would recognise him

while cycling again, and can give a good description of his general appearance and of the bicycle. It was an old roadster with a rear mudguard which rattled when the bike went over bumps and rough patches. We might be able to pick that bike up before it's repaired, and it might — " Wilson broke off, as if suddenly undecided what to say, but at last added in a helpless kind of way: "I just feel that it's my lucky day, George. I think we should put out a general call in the West and North-West area for any information about a cyclist with a loose rear mudguard seen between two-thirty and three-thirty, say — perhaps up to four o'clock this morning. Will you okay it to *Information*? I'll do the rest, Commander, if you'll just say the word."

"I'll do it right away," promised Gideon without hesitation. "I'll have you put through to *Information* and I'll talk to them on the other telephone, at the same time."

"Thanks!" crowed Wilson.

Gideon put the receiver down while Hobbs began to dial on the internal telephone. As he gave instructions, Gideon was most affected by Wilson's obvious delight and enthusiasm. There was that to be glad about as well as the remarkable beginning of the young Police Constable Oswald. And Archer, Hobbs — oh, there was so much to be thankful for!

For a few moments, at least, the shadow of what might happen if racial conflict should erupt over London lifted. He was just a policeman, doing his job.

Chapter 12
THE BICYCLE

DAVID WELLS took his cycle from the cement cycle-rack provided at a garage close to Ealing Common Station, and began what was usually his most peaceful and quiet fifteen minutes: cycling home. There was something almost remote about riding on a bicycle in the midst of noisy, fussy, smelly motor-traffic, and a sense of being absolutely alone. He had enjoyed cycling since his boyhood and it was no sacrifice to him that he could not afford to run a car. He hired or borrowed one for the summer holiday, and for an occasional weekend, so as to give all the family a treat. But driving made him irritable, whereas cycling gave him peace.

He always went the long way home, across Ealing Common with its well-kept and well-trimmed trees and well-marked roads, with large houses still privately owned as well as some new and exclusive apartment blocks where old houses had been demolished by bomb or the demolitioners' machines. Tonight was calm, and, perhaps because he was a little late, there was less traffic about. Soon, he was in the maze of narrower streets and heading towards home.

He felt a strange and unfamiliar tension, hating the thought of facing Ellen, who was bound to have heard about the murder by now. Yet what he had done, surely, he had done for her. He was oblivious of the twisted thinking in this reasoning and saw it simply as a fact: to save her from anguish, to keep the family together, he had murdered Rosamund.

But oh God! How he kept on seeing Rosamund's face!

How he could picture the photograph of her in the *Evening News*, which was folded and thrust into the canvas saddlebag which touched the loose-fitting rear mudguard.

For weeks he had been meaning to have that mudguard fixed and the saddlebag raised. However the one needed soldering and the other should have two extra holes punched in the straps, and each was time-consuming and easy to put off. He had so little time, what with seeing so much of

Rosamund, and spending a reasonable amount at home and working five and a half days a week. He cycled on and cycled well, very upright on the saddle, shoulders squared and unmoving, his legs from his hips down doing the work.

It did not occur to him, in the anonymous world of the bicycle, that the noise of saddlebag and mudguard was most distinctive and most noticeable once one became aware of it.

A policeman at Ealing Common Station, looking out for a bicycle which made such a noise, was acutely aware of this one when it passed during a lull in the motor-traffic. He telephoned Divisional Headquarters who sent out a general alert throughout the Division. Utterly oblivious of this, David Wells put the bicycle in the shed at the back of his house, which was in two flats, his being the ground floor. Hearing Leonard, the younger boy, whining, he hesitated outside the back door.

He couldn't stand that tonight; he simply couldn't stand it.

But he had to.

Then the door opened and Lennie came hurrying, tear-stained but beaming, wanting only to be lifted shoulder high, and so encouraged to burst out into a giggle of laughter. As he ducked the lintel so as not to knock the child's head, there was a welcome aroma of frying sausages and bacon, always a favourite of his. And Ellen had obviously washed and curled her hair and brushed gloss into it: she looked younger, less careworn, eager to see him, but not overpowering him with hugs and kisses.

Soon he was eating, while she was frying bread in the fat from the bacon.

"Dear," she said, "something very nice happened to Judy Wallace today." Judy was the wife of the man who lived in the upper flat. "You know she lost her engagement ring two months ago, when we had that burglary?"

He remembered; there had been nothing worth stealing in here.

"Yes," he said, wiping off some fat which dribbled down his chin.

"She's going to get it back! The police had her description of it, and it was found early this morning. A policeman was here early this afternoon — "

At the word "police" he went into a spasm of panic. He couldn't help it, it simply happened. He sat holding his knife and fork poised, much as he had sat at the office, his heart thumping and the rest of his body cold and still.

But Ellen's back was towards him, the bread sizzled, Lennie was preoccupied with a toy lion, and no one noticed anything amiss. Wells had not the faintest idea that he broke out of the strange trauma at the very moment that a policeman at the end of Caerphilly Street was reporting to two policemen in a patrol car:

"There's a bicycle answering the one described belonging to a David Wells, at Flat 1, Number 27 Gill Street. And the back mudguard is loose. I followed him from the Broadway . . ."

* * *

When P.C. Oswald was told this, an hour or two later, he said with absolute confidence: "If I could see him riding after dark, sir, I'd recognise him."

"I certainly hope you can," said Superintendent Wilson. "There's something else you will be interested to hear, Oswald."

"What's that, sir?" Oswald was eager, but had emerged from the period of excitement, not far removed from elation, which had possessed him for so much of the day.

"A cyclist was seen by another of our men coming from the direction of the house where Rosamund Lee's body was found, about three o'clock last night. And the rear mudguard rattled a bit. We shall keep the house and man under observation, and the next time he goes out on his bicycle at night I want you to see him. Be ready to come at a moment's notice. If you go out anywhere, see that the Station knows where to find you."

"I'll make quite sure I do, sir." Oswald tried to keep the elation out of his voice.

Had a raw policeman ever got off to a better start?

* * *

Ellen Wells, forcing herself to be bright and gay, somehow keeping the children quiet, somehow eating a little although food nearly choked her, knew that she was failing, that something was badly wrong. She couldn't bear it if David left her for another woman, she really couldn't bear it.

She simply couldn't stand being left to cope on her own.

Upstairs, in a newly-decorated, newly-furnished flat, one of the most contemporary near Caerphilly Street, dark-haired, bright-eyed, full-lipped Judy Wallace was holding her left hand out in front of her face, turning it right and turning it left for an imaginary diamond ring to catch the light and so scintillate. She had never thought she would see the engagement ring again, she could not get over the fact that when all the formalities were over she would actually get it back.

Her husband, son of an Englishman and his Italian wife, was dark-haired and handsome in a Southern European way. He cupped her breasts in his hands, drawing her closer and closer, putting his lips to her ear and nibbling the lobe gently, his eyes following the movement of the hand, his cheek moving until he rubbed it gently against hers. As she leaned back against him catching his mood, he whispered:

"I think we ought to celebrate, sweetheart. *Now*, too."

"But Ray, supper — "

"I said *now*."

She suddenly spun round and hugged and kissed him open-mouthed.

"Don't blame me if you feel hungry!"

He put his hand to the little tag at the zipper at the back of her dress.

* * *

That was the moment when Saxby stepped from Hobbs's office into Gideon's, where Hobbs was already standing by the window. Saxby, with his pear-shaped face and body looked both pale and tired. Dust and tiny pieces of rubble had settled on his hair, arms and shoulders. His eyes widened when he saw the whisky and soda, and he looked at it with such longing that Hobbs poured out a two-finger drink as he sat down.

"Well, Mark," Gideon said. "What's on your mind?"

"It's time I retired and made way for younger men," Saxby growled. "Ah. Cheers." He actually smacked his lips. "Commander, I've goofed. Badly. There *is* a kind of Black Power organisation in my manor. Archer, my second-in-command, has kept on nagging me about it and I've kept telling him we want more proof. Well, now we've got it."

"Because of the Lancelot Place affair?" asked Gideon.

"No. Much more. We went to the home of one of the ring-leaders of the attack on Rataudi's house. It's a room at the back of a café where they sell Pakistani, Indian and Jamaican snacks as well as fried fish and chips and chicken and chips. We found enough documents there to show that Archer is absolutely right. The Black Power group has hundreds of members, and the only objective is to make as much trouble as possible. We got a copy of their rules but not the names and addresses of the members. The immigrants are seething. Even the most liberal and tolerant have lost their patience. Seven of their people were killed in today's collapse and they want revenge — on Rataudi and his partners, on every profiteering landlord in London. And tonight could be flashpoint. We've never needed every man on duty as we do tonight." He tossed down his whisky and soda. "I hadn't come to that conclusion when I telephoned you, George. I feel sick about the whole business. It was something young Archer said when I left which really started me thinking." He drew a deep breath and faced Gideon as squarely as a man could, as if this were a

179

kind of confessional. "He asked me to consider having an all night stand-by alert in the Division, with concentrations of men on duty in all areas with a large immigrant population. And he suggested special watch on the houses of known profiteering landlords. That told me how desperate *he* thinks the situation has become, George. And I'm afraid I've left it too late."

Gideon could imagine exactly how Saxby was feeling; even worse, he himself was touched with anxiety that the others may be right. He stretched forward and pulled the file towards him and flipped over documents until he came to an outline map of the Division and parts of those adjoining. Hobbs joined them at the desk. There were small areas shaded in black, including the Notting Hill district close to Long Street. Some areas were shaded grey, some remained white. The neighbouring Divisions had their share of black and grey also.

Black showed a heavy concentration of immigrants.

Grey showed a concentration of much less density.

White, ironically, showed areas which

were only where white people lived.

There flashed through his mind a sense of anger, that there should be such Divisions, that such a situation had ever been allowed to develop, but that was not the immediate problem: meeting the present situation mattered. He looked up to find Hobbs's eyes close to his.

"There's time to stop the change of shift in the Divisions," Hobbs said. "Time to allow everyone an hour off before we put them on stand-by. We can organise a meal up in the canteen if we arrange for extra staff in the cafeteria. Will you speak to *Uniform*, sir, and see what help they can give? I'll brief all our chaps."

So Hobbs had no doubt that Archer was right; nor, for that matter, had Gideon.

"I'll talk to *Uniform*," he promised. He thought that if *Uniform* raised any difficulties, either of protest or availability of men, he would go straight over their heads to Scott-Marle. But he didn't expect, nor did he get, any obstructiveness. If anything, he sensed that the Commander of the Uniformed Branch wondered why this request had been so long in coming. When it was all done, Saxby looked younger by ten years. He, Gideon, and Hobbs felt some measure of satisfaction, but there was one great cause for anxiety: the landlords. Some were known and could be protected, but a great number, living in different parts of London, were not known to the police but might be to the Black Power group. Obviously each one was in danger, those quite innocent of over-crowding and profiteering as well as the guilty.

Rataudi might know many of them.

After all the emergency arrangements were made, Gideon looked at his watch. It was nearly twenty to seven, and he immediately went along to the waiting rooms. He had left Mahommet Rataudi kicking his heels for a long time, certainly long enough to have made any Englishman complain; but Rataudi showed no sign of impatience or distress. He had some evening newspapers whose front pages carried huge headlines and some remarkable pictures of the collapsing wall, including one of Riddell actually being buried. He had also some newspapers in Bengali, thin and poorly printed on greyish paper, and folded small enough to go into his pocket. He stood up, pressed the tips of his fingers together and bowed slightly. He looked neither young nor old, but ageless; neither good nor bad, but touched with suffering.

"Sorry I've kept you," Gideon said. "It's going to be a busy night and it's been a very hard day."

"For that, sir, I am deeply sorry," Rataudi said.

"What are you prepared to do to make amends?" Gideon asked.

"Commander Gideon," replied Rataudi, with dignity, "I feel no responsibility and no guilt, and so no need to make amends." He added a few words in his own tongue and Gideon detected the name "Allah" uttered several times. "But of course I am prepared to help in any way I can all these unfortunate people of my country."

Gideon, eyeing him very directly, avoided argument and said:

"There are indications of serious outbreaks of violence. You, your partners and other landlords of overcrowded property are in acute danger. Before we can protect all of you we must know who and where the others are. You can at least name your partners." He waited but Rataudi said neither yes nor no. "Can you name others whom the crowd might attack?" he demanded.

"Are the police *so* helpless?" asked Rataudi, suddenly, and he made it sound like a simple question with no implications.

"We can protect you and others if we know where you are," Gideon said. "We can't if we don't." He waited for a few moments and got no response, so he went on: "Mr. Rataudi, I shall have to investigate the conditions at Long Street to find out whether any law was broken. Whether you and other landlords like the idea or not there will have to be a very thorough investigation, possibly by a Court of Inquiry. I would rather be able to improve the situation now, and not wait until there has been a lot of violence and so arrests and court cases. That would only make a bad situation worse."

He feared that Rataudi was going to refuse to help, even as he spoke. He had a strange feeling, that he was not really communicating with the man, that Rataudi was facing an ultimatum for which he saw no justification. It was as if he and the Pakistani came not only from different countries but from different worlds.

Then, Rataudi said in a tired-sounding voice: "I will give you some names and addresses, Commander. You understand, of course, that I do not know them all. If I may have a pen and some paper on which to write..."

* * *

Before dark, the police had dozens of houses under guard — the home of every landlord they knew to be in danger from mob violence. Some were in the over-crowded areas, some in residential sub-urbs, a few in beautiful houses in the West End, Knightsbridge, Kensington and Hampstead. A dozen attacks began, but were all abortive, for the ringleaders had not expected to find police ready for them. Patrol cars were available for reinforce-ments, but none was needed.

Protest meetings were held at the ap-proaches to Long Street and to all other predominantly immigrant areas. There were threats to profiteering landlords and demands for equality between black and white. Protest marches were hurriedly organised, but all were easily contained. It was an uneasy night but a victory, at least by stalemate, for the police.

While much of this was going on, Gideon was at home with Honiwell, sitting in the kitchen eating a mountain of sausages and chips which Penny had cooked. She had gone out and the two men were soon on their own in the big front room, whisky between them hardly touched, Honiwell fiddling with a cigar which kept going out. They had discussed the Entwhistle case in detail, and now Gideon had to advise the other man what to do. Despite the standby alert throughout the whole of the London area, Gideon's whole attention was concentrated on the problem of Entwhistle, his children, and Eric Greenwood.

And one possibility was growing in his mind: that what a man had done once, he might do again. Greenwood's growing list of mistresses and what seemed to be the intensity of his latest affair with a merchant seaman's wife appeared to be leading to a crisis of some kind. The worsening mental condition of Entwhistle at Dartmoor and reports which came in about his children, particularly the girl Carol, demanded action for another, very strong reason.

On the table between their two armchairs was a report from detective sergeant Benbow, who had been assigned exclusively to this reinvestigation. It read:

"The aunt with whom the children are living reports that the two eldest, Clive and Jennifer, are apparently no longer troubled although occasionally each is mocked at school with taunts of being the child of a killer. Such phrases as: 'Your Dad killed your Mum, didn't he?' are less common but still liable to be used at any time. The child Carol is much more affected by these taunts than the others. Always more distressed, being more sensitive by nature, she is 'lonely and withdrawn', to quote a form mistress at her school as well as the aunt. The aunt has recently discovered an illustrated tourist book on Devon hidden in the children's bedroom. Carol had pasted in snapshots of her mother and father opposite a picture of Dartmoor Prison. The eldest child, Clive, might remember if Greenwood ever visited the home while the father was away and, if he recognised Greenwood, might enable us to break the man down."

Gideon picked it up, and said. "Matt, we've a very awkward problem. Certainly we may have to use the boy Clive, but only as confirmation, not as a means of breaking Greenwood's confidence. If we make any move and are wrong, it could put an end to all Entwhistle's hopes and that might do both Entwhistle and the child irretrievable harm. On the other hand we can't reopen the case officially — which means publicly — simply because of the mental condition of father or child. We can only reopen it if we are absolutely certain of our case against Greenwood — but remember we were once certain of our case against Entwhistle. If this were a new case we could move on circumstantial evidence, but we need much more before we can reopen an old one."

Honiwell simply raised his hands helplessly, and Gideon touched another report, a detailed one of Greenwood's amorous adventures.

"We could tackle Greenwood if we had reason to believe that he might do the same thing again, but no matter what we think, we can't take action of any kind without very strong evidence that he killed Margaret Entwhistle. As far as I can see the only proof we can get after this lapse of time is a confession and the only hope of getting a confession seems to be by presenting Greenwood with strong circumstantial evidence." He took out his pipe and began to polish it with the palm of his right hand. "Is there any such evidence?"

After a long pause, Honiwell answered: "Not yet, George."

"Then I don't see how we can act until we have some. Is there really any hope of your sergeant getting it?"

"He's turned up a surprising lot of stuff," answered Honiwell. "I think he might find what we want, but I'm damned if I think he'll find it in time." His voice seemed to echo in the big, old-fashioned room, when a police car pulled up outside. The curtains weren't drawn; Gideon saw the driver get out and wondered what this was about. He could imagine only an emergency, yet if it were one, why hadn't he been telephoned? His mind sprang at once to news about the standby alarm, but suddenly he saw Kate get out of the police car and heard her clear:

"Thank you very much. Good-night."

She came briskly towards the front door as the car moved off.

* * *

Detective sergeant Sam Benbow sat in a small, cellar restaurant in King's Road, Chelsea, enjoying good, solid Belgian cooking and a low-priced but nicely dry Moselle, just right for the rather fatty stuffed veal. He had a corner table and a newspaper propped up so that he could read all the details of the murder at Ealing and of the disaster at Notting Hill. He looked much more like a boxer than a policeman, had one cauliflower ear, a broken nose and flattened lips. It wasn't until one looked into his bright, periwinkle blue eyes that one began to trust him.

The woman who hustled two blue-smocked Finnish-speaking waitresses about, bustled to and from the kitchen, which her husband ruled, and took all the orders in good, if obviously accented, English. When she came to offer Benbow another slice of veal, or more sauté potatoes, he kissed her hand in an extravagant gesture.

"Wonderful!" he boomed. "Wonderful!" As she served him he took a photograph out of his breast pocket, one of Eric Greenwood. "Don't happen to know him, do you?"

She looked down, and shook her head.

"I do not see him, ever," she answered, and piled the potatoes high.

Benbow, who was married to a woman who was out night after night on social work in the East End, put the photograph away. Five nights a week he visited a different restaurant in this part of London, for one of the things Bessie Smith had said in passing was that Greenwood liked to eat in this area, where food was less expensive yet often as good as in Soho and the West End.

Five times the *patron* had recognised Greenwood, but none had recognised Margaret Entwhistle as well. Somewhere in London, Benbow believed, he would find someone who recognised them both. True, it was a long time ago, but the human mind could be remarkably retentive, and the owners and head waiters of small restaurants would often remember not only faces but food likes and dislikes over several years.

The one positive thing emerging was that Eric Greenwood, in his way, was very much a Don Juan.

* * *

Also on his travels was Simon Goodenough. And as he travelled so much and to far places, he had greater opportunity than most men. He accepted only one obligation to his wife — apart from keeping her, of course! — he made quite sure that he had caught no venereal disease, so that whenever he was home with her nothing was barred. Perhaps because they were apart so often, when he was home their life was tumultuous and wildly exciting. He wasn't sure that out of all his "conquests" his wife didn't give him most pleasure.

At the back of his mind he knew that when he was at sea, she had lovers, but this was a forbidden subject even to him. Provided she was at home, waiting, eager for him, he was happy. At the moment when Sam Benbow had shown Greenwood's photograph to the Belgian woman he was on the bridge of the *Orianda*, thinking about Jennifer, longing to be back.

CHAPTER 13

STAND-BY

"I MUST be off," said Honiwell, as the front door of Gideon's house opened.

"Don't rush," urged Gideon.

"Hallo, George," Kate called as she opened the front door with her key.

Gideon went into the passage to welcome her, a gesture which Honiwell noticed with a sharp pang. He wanted to talk in confidence to Gideon about his situation with Netta, but this broke across his mood, and would almost certainly change Gideon's. Outside, Kate put her cheek forward to be kissed, and Gideon hugged her for a moment, very tightly. As he let her go, he said:

"Have you had supper?"

"All I need, dear," she answered, "except for some coffee — or tea, as it's so late. Did I see another head in the front room?"

"Matt Honiwell's here," Gideon told her, and they stepped into the big room. Honiwell was already on his feet in front of his chair. There were brief greetings, before Gideon went on: "How's Vi Riddell, Kate?"

Kate was taking off a close-fitting hat, and poking her fingers into her greying hair, which was a little flattened and yet still attractive. It gave her a rakish look.

"Do you know, I'm not really sure," she answered seriously. "Much better than I would have expected in some ways. Almost as if — " Kate paused, one hand at her side now, the other holding her hat in front of her breast — "as if she's relieved."

"Relieved!" echoed Honiwell.

"Yes, that's why I'm puzzled. She said that she's been worried about Jim for a long time. Apparently he was near a breakdown before his holiday, and if he hadn't gone away she thinks he would have collapsed. She told me a lot I hadn't expected, too — but you don't want to hear about it now, you must have something to discuss with Matt."

"I'd like to know, too," Honiwell said. "So will Netta. She took a liking to Vi Riddell last night. My God, only *last* night," he almost groaned. "You've packed a week in this day, George!"

"Well, briefly then," conceded Kate a little reluctantly. "Violet Riddell's been very worried about Riddell, who was obsessed by the fact that he simply couldn't see the racial problem objectively. First his sympathies were all on her side, then they swung round to the other. She wasn't able to help him. Once he used to talk about his problems to her but he's hardly talked at all about this. She thinks he needs to talk to someone and that's been her only way to help him, just letting him talk. Now, she longs to get him home so that she can nurse him and start making him confide in her again." Putting her hand on Gideon's shoulder, Kate went on: "She's sure he would have cracked up mentally if something hadn't happened. Now, provided he gets over this — " Kate's fingers tightened on Gideon's shoulder. "George, he's all she lives for, and I promised to keep her in touch with the latest news. He *will* get over it, won't he ?"

There was no way of being sure about recovery, Gideon knew. He had learned before leaving his office that Riddell had already had an emergency operation because of internal haemorrhage from crushing and there was after all some cerebral haemorrhage. No surgeon would predict how he would get on. That was all he could tell Kate, and all she could tell Vi Riddell, on the telephone. When she finished, she picked up her hat from the sideboard and moved towards the door.

"I'll bring some tea," she said. "Or would you rather have coffee, Matt?"

"Coffee, please," Honiwell opted.

When Kate had gone out of the room, Gideon looked at the other man with a different kind of appraisal. He had watched him as Kate had talked, and sensed that Honiwell was affected by the story; he also recalled the way he had said: "Netta will want to know, too. She took a liking to Vi Riddell last night." There was nothing more to discuss over the Entwhistle/Greenwood affair, which could hardly be more unsatisfactory, and until reports came in, nothing more could be done about the stand-by. As always, Kate had comforted him, and it was Gideon the human being rather than Gideon the detective who now faced Honiwell whose features were shadowed by a dark-green lampshade.

"Good occasions, these dinner-dances,"

Gideon remarked. "Kate hadn't met Netta before. She took to her as Netta obviously took to Violet Riddell. How long have you known Netta now ?"

Honiwell leaned forward in his chair so that his face caught the light on one side; his features were not particularly good but he had a generous-looking mouth and his hair, in need of cutting, was more like a child's than a man's. He did look rather like a huge, cuddly stuffed toy or dummy.

"Just over two years," he said. "George, I'd like to talk on a personal matter, if you can bear it."

"Fire away," urged Gideon.

"It isn't so easy."

"Personal matters seldom are," said Gideon, and he smiled. "Get it off your chest, Matt. You joined the Force only about two years after me — I was your first sergeant. Remember ?"

"My God, so you were!" he exclaimed. "I made a bloody fool of myself over a prostitute, tackled her on her own and when you came along she was yelling her head off telling the world I was trying to rape her."

"Only I'd seen her before," Gideon said, laughter in his voice.

"If you'd been some stuck-up basket God knows where that would have landed me," said Honiwell. He was smiling broadly, but gradually sobered. "That's a long time ago. Twenty-seven years."

"Yes."

"I can't say I've regretted a day of it," said Honiwell, "except — George, do you remember the Singleton bother out in Thames Division? Damn fool question. You were there. I doubt if you know that I was."

"Do you mean when Singleton nearly killed his wife's boy-friend?"

"Yes."

"It would be hard to forget," said Gideon, musingly. He knew that the question must indicate what subject was on Honiwell's mind, for a man had been tried and sentenced and was now in gaol, and Gideon himself had chosen to give evidence against him, while feeling great compassion. "What are you driving at, Matt?"

Honiwell gulped.

"Nothing we'd like to do more, but Netta

and I can't get married for years. Indefi-
nitely."

"Oh," Gideon said. "I'm sorry."

"Her husband won't divorce her, and the
new law doesn't apply to her yet."

"Breakdown in her marriage, you mean."

"Yes."

"How are you tackling the situation?"
asked Gideon.

"We're living together."

"I certainly can't say I blame you,"
Gideon said, and Honiwell's eyes lit up.

"Do you mean that?"

"Of course I mean it."

"George," said Honiwell. "The police
have to give a good example."

"You do," retorted Gideon.

"George," repeated Honiwell, obviously
with a greater effort, "I'm deeply troubled
about this."

"Matt," Gideon said, "I don't think you
need be. You're not pretending to be
married, are you — haven't been through
any ceremony?"

"Good God, no!"

"Then if you and Netta think this is
right for you, what's bothering you?"
asked Gideon.

He knew, of course, with not the slightest doubt. But if he allowed Honiwell to realise that then he, Gideon, would have made it appear glaringly obvious that there was cause for anxiety; that was the very last thing he wanted to do. So he looked blandly at Honiwell, who drew in a deep breath before asking:

"You really don't see?"

"No."

"Then it can't be as bad as I thought it was," Honiwell said, and when Gideon didn't comment, he went on: "I could come up against the Press, or I could run into a case where the defence knows about me and Netta, or finds out. I can't keep it secret, George. I'll bet a dozen little pip-squeaks know about it and it's all over the place now. If I charge any of the old lags, anyone with a record, they'll dig it out and sell it to the Press. If it was juicy enough, there are a lot of newspapers which would use it. Er — take this case, George."

A little more heavily, as if he were just beginning to understand, Gideon said:

"Entwhistle and Greenwood?"

"Of course."

"I see what you mean," said Gideon,

thoughtfully. "If you're the man who re-opens the case and a newspaper gets word of your relationship with Netta, the story would be irresistible; police officer who is living out of wedlock spends months track-ing down a man who murdered a woman he had been living with. Or who'd been his mistress, anyhow." Gideon rubbed his chin, very slowly, and made a rasping noise with his stubble. He hoped Kate wouldn't come in yet, this was something he wanted to finish with Honiwell alone, and he had now seen more clearly than he had before: in this particular case Honiwell was vulnerable, and it was possible that one or more newspapers would give the angle headlines. There was at least one which lost no opportunity to get in a crack at the Yard.

He heard cups rattle.

"George," said Honiwell, huskily, "you're beginning to see what I mean, aren't you?"

"Yes," said Gideon, and got up and went to the door. "Kate," he called, seeing her at the end of the passage with a tray in her hands. "Give us another ten minutes, will you?"

"Of course," Kate called back.

Gideon turned back into the room and now stood looking down on this man whom he had known for so long, and who had served the Yard so well. From this angle, Honiwell seemed older: not tired, just older — and anxious and perhaps even disillusioned.

"Yes," Gideon repeated. "Now that I've allied it to the Entwhistle/Greenwood case, I see exactly what you mean. That's not the problem. The problem is to make you understand exactly what I think." Now he sat on the arm of his chair and the chair tilted a little. "I think that whatever sneers or scandal some of the Press might use, you would convince a jury absolutely of your integrity — just as you have always convinced me. I think that every man who matters at the Yard, from Scott-Marle downwards, would be behind you: you have to live your life in the happiest way you can. You might get some cracks from newspapers and neighbours, but you wouldn't get any from the Yard. I am absolutely convinced of that."

Honiwell's eyes were glowing, and he was breathing very hard. The house and the street seemed quiet, and the quiet was accentuated when a car flashed passed the window and the sound quickly died away.

"And I'll tell you something else," Gideon went on. "Kate would agree with me absolutely. You and Netta will always be welcome here. I'll give her the gist of the situation afterwards." He stood up and, in a rare gesture, placed a hand on Honiwell's shoulder. "Matt, you may find neighbours difficult at times, you may run into technical problems such as when you travel, but you won't have any trouble at the Yard. My Goodness," he exclaimed, "just think of Rollo and his reputation! Compared with him, you're as white as driven snow!"

* * *

Gideon told Kate the story when they were getting ready for bed, and she reacted as he had expected although warning him that there might be more disapproval than he expected. But he had the satisfaction of knowing that he had sent Honiwell off very much happier than when he arrived. The Entwhistle case troubled him, but against this was the silent telephone, the increasing confidence that all had gone well on this night of stand-by, when every policeman in London was ready for an emergency call.

It was half-past seven when he woke. He heard the milk float in the street, heard a boy whistling, thought he heard Penny on the landing. He got out of bed without disturbing Kate, put on his camel hair dressing-gown which made him look huge around the middle, pushed his feet into wool-lined leather slippers, last year's Christmas present from Priscilla and her husband: they were trodden down badly at the heels. Outside, he found Penny on the landing between her room and the bathroom, looking up towards the loft hatch, rather wistfully. She was so pretty in a fluffy, pink and white dressing-gown, her hair tumbling about her shoulders; these days she usually wore it with a bun at the nape of her neck, a Victorian fashion back in favour. She had obviously just come out of the bathroom, her cheeks and nose were shiny.

"No," Gideon said, "I haven't forgotten."

She jumped round. "Oh, Daddy! You scared me."

205

"I broke a daydream, didn't I?" her father asked. "And a slightly reproachful mood about your father, who promised to have the loft sound-proofed so that you could practise your piano without disturbing the neighbours, and hasn't done a thing about it."

Penny flushed, but did not avert her gaze.

"I was wondering when you would be able to get round to it. But I know how busy you are, and there isn't really any hurry."

But there was, of course; all youth was impatient. He saw how she checked an impulse to move closer to him; she wouldn't want to cosset him to help persuade. So he moved forward himself and gave her a hug with one arm.

"I've had an expert out to look over it," he told her. "He said it can be done, the biggest problem is going to be to get the piano up there. He's going to estimate and if we come to terms, the work will be started in the New Year and will take about a month."

She didn't speak, but looked ravishingly radiant; she didn't fling herself at him, boisterous and child-like, but just huddled against him; he could feel her firm bosom and the throbbing life. He thought of Hobbs; he felt the pressure of her arms and a choky: "Oh, Daddy, thank you." Then he stood her away from him, so disturbingly aware of her, his youngest daughter; and he thought of no one else in the world. How she must have longed for this news; how difficult, despite her full life, the waiting must have been.

* * *

At the time when Gideon was standing on the landing with Penelope, Carol Entwhistle was sitting with her brother and sister, eating cornflakes liberally swamped in milk and sprinkled with brown sugar. Her aunt, so tall and grave and concerned, did not show special concern for her but in fact was much more troubled than for a long time past. Yet Carol ate more heartily than usual, and for once was ready to leave for school before the others. She was by the kitchen door, satchel over her shoulder packed very tightly, school beret on, blue raincoat on.

"Auntie, may I go on ahead?" she asked.

"I'd like to look in the library at school before the crowd comes."

"Yes, pet," her aunt agreed, and moved over and gave her a kiss on the cheek. "Off you go."

So Carol went off.

Her aunt would not expect to see her again until four o'clock or later, for she lunched at school like the other two. She moved sedately, as always, fifteen minutes ahead of time.

But instead of going to school, she caught a bus; she felt confident that her aunt didn't know that instead of books she had some clothes, a toothbrush and her toilet necessities in her satchel, together with all her savings, every penny. There was over ten pounds. She felt sure that she had enough money to get to Dartmoor.

She simply *had* to see her father.

CHAPTER 14
BRIEFING

GIDEON turned into his office at a few minutes after nine that morning, to find a pile of new reports and half a dozen messages under a paper knife which Kate had given him, oh, it must have been twenty years ago. And there were the morning's newspapers, folded across the middle and placed neatly in front of one another. He put his heavy overcoat on a clothes-stand, and just glanced out of the window, at a dull grey Thames and a leaden sky. Brrh! It was cold enough for snow! He crossed to the desk, sat down, and put the paper knife aside.

The newspapers carried huge photographs of the disaster, of Riddell the police hero, of Rataudi; and the leading articles, which Gideon glanced at, were full of fulmination against "authorities who permitted and landlords who abused the situation".

The first message was from Hobbs. "Rollo will be here at ten o'clock, Piluski at

209

half-past ten. Rollo knows what you want him for, Piluski doesn't."

Gideon put that aside.

The next was from Scott-Marle's secretary. "The Commissioner would like a report on the Notting Hill incident" — incident! thought Gideon — "at two o'clock, please. As detailed as possible, as it is needed for a conference at three o'clock."

Gideon pursed his lips and reflected that such requests usually came through the Assistant Commissioner, it really did look as if Scott-Marle was making him double his own job with the A.C.'s. An issue was going to be forced about that before long, he could see it coming. He pushed the message aside but not out of his mind, and found an envelope, sealed and marked "Personal". He didn't recognise the writing but opened it with the paper knife and unfolded a single sheet of notepaper. There were two words: "Thanks. Matt." He smiled briefly and picked up the next message and read with deep satisfaction: "Chief Superintendent Riddell had a good night. He is still in the intensive care ward but the post-surgical report is satisfactory."

For the first time Gideon sat back and

stared out of the window, recollection of what Kate had told him about Vi Riddell passing through his mind.

That was all the messages, but the Post, Inwards tray was very full, and he ran through the contents. Letters from divisions and other Police Forces, mostly inviting him to special functions; letters requesting co-operation from the Yard with Sydney, Australia, Buenos Aires, Cape Town and Vienna. There were two charity appeals and a variety of mail order offers. Before he finished he dialled the typing pool, and asked:

"Is Miss Sale there and free?"

"Yes, sir."

"Ask her to come and see Commander Gideon."

"Very good, sir."

Sabrina knew him better than anyone in the pool and could answer most of his letters for him; he had to get them in hand now or they wouldn't be done until the afternoon which meant that they probably wouldn't get off today. He made pencilled notes for her guidance, then turned to the case reports. The top one was about the murder of young Rosamund Lee, at Ealing.

He opened and read Hobbs's comments:

The suspect did not use his bicycle last night so the constable, Oswald, was not able to see him. This suspect, David Wells, is under constant but secret surveillance. No immediate action needed.

The next report was also from the Ealing area, from EF Division. It confirmed the value of the recovered jewels at £60,000 and added: "Both accused will appear this morning at the West London Police Court. The antique dealer has not yet been caught." And again Hobbs recommended: "No immediate action needed."

There was a tap at the door, he called "Come in" and Sabrina Sale entered. She was, as always, neatly dressed and nicely made-up, and he noticed that her hair had a faint tint of blue. Her glasses were inconspicuous, her voice pleasant. He thought of her dancing with Rollo, wondering again how well she knew him, as he waved her to a chair and she sat down and crossed her very nice legs; her skirt was just above her knees. There was a minimum of "Good mornings" as she handed him the letters typed by the girl who had taken his dictation yesterday; at a glance, these seemed well spaced and typed. After a word about the Ball, he plunged into what he wanted Sabrina to do, and passed over the file.

"Just run through this lot while I sign these and read my reports, will you ?"

"Of course." She leaned forward, the lace of her blouse making a little flurry of movement; he was very aware of her figure.

He picked up the next few reports. There was a full one about the post office robbery, and here Hobbs recommended: "You might be well advised to see Ringall today." So he put that folder aside. It was ten minutes before he had finished reading all the files, and so far as he could judge he had absorbed the essentials of them all. Some time during the day he would talk with Hobbs about them. He put the last files aside and looked up, well aware that Sabrina Sale was watching him intently.

"Any problems ?" he asked.

"Not among these letters, Commander," she answered.

"But still problems," he observed.

"I think so," said Sabrina. "Commander — I've never made any comment to you about the correspondence or about any case going through the Yard, have I?"

"No," he agreed, and wondered what was to come.

"May I now?"

"You may if you wish."

"Thank you," she said. The fact that she wasn't smiling told him she was really serious, and he had never seen her in earnest before. "I think the Notting Hill affair will cause terrible trouble, perhaps a disaster, unless those responsible are brought to book very quickly."

He went still; she did not avert her gaze.

"Go on," he said.

"And whereas until now the more level-headed and moderate immigrants have not wanted to take part in demonstrations, after yesterday many of them do. They feel that they have been victimised far too long."

"I see," he said. "Why are you so sure about this?"

"Because I know a great number of them," she answered. "I've lived as a neighbour for a long time. One of the men who has been working terribly hard to try to assimilate the immigrants into some districts says that nine out of ten members of a committee which met last night have changed their attitudes from non-intervention to immediate intervention." Sabrina seemed to colour under Gideon's direct gaze but she went on: "I'm afraid I'm putting this very badly."

"Are you saying that the non-militants among them are likely to become strikingly militant if there isn't some very quick action?"

"That's exactly what I mean," she agreed. "And — " She broke off.

"Don't pull any punches," Gideon said drily.

"Have no fears, Commander! I think there are already far more militants among them than is healthy." When Gideon didn't comment, she went on: "I'm really scared. I really am."

"Of what might happen?"

"Of what will happen if there is any attempt to smooth this over," she corrected.

Gideon leaned back in his chair as Big Ben began to chime, and this meant that it was ten o'clock. There wasn't time to keep Rollo waiting; this morning was going to be too crowded for any delays but he wanted to make Sabrina realise that he understood and was as anxious as she to act quickly. He also wanted to make her understand that there was nothing simple about the task.

"Sabrina," he asked. "Do you really mean they want a scapegoat?"

"No," she answered. "What I really mean is that they think the overcrowding is criminal, that what happened yesterday is murder, and that even the nicest among them are bitterly angry." She leaned forward, one hand outstretched; he noticed how beautifully the hand was kept. "Just a statement that the police are treating it as a murder inquiry, or even manslaughter, would help. They — they *mustn't* be allowed to explode."

Her cheeks had gone red in her vehemence, and Gideon was sure that she felt that she had failed to make her point and was disappointed and frustrated. Perhaps to her, certainly to his own surprise, he leaned forward and covered her hand with his.

"If this business is mishandled," he said clearly, "it could create one of the ugliest situations we've ever had in London. You're seeing only the one side, you know. We have to see the situation as it is, not as we'd like it to be, not from one angle only. There is a very strong anti-immigrant movement. It is not simply political but it has its right-wing extremists. If we take the wrong course of action, we could provoke and infuriate them as much as the other side has already incited them, and our job — the job of the police — is to keep the peace." He gave her hand a little squeeze, then withdrew his own. "Have no doubt at all, we are treating this as a matter of utmost gravity. There is to be a conference of V.I.P.s at three o'clock this afternoon. Our anxiety — like yours — is that other people won't see the danger, particularly the Government Departments concerned. We *can* only act as policemen."

As he finished, not sure how Sabrina Sale was taking all this, there was a buzz from Hobbs's office — the extension on the inter-office machine. He lifted it, and went on to Sabrina:

"This conference is at the highest level.

Don't have the slightest doubt that we are taking it very seriously indeed."

She said huskily: "I should — I should have known. I'm sorry. May I — may I tell my friends that ?"

"Of course," Gideon said.

"Thank you very much." Sabrina picked up the signed letters and the reports and turned away as Gideon lifted the receiver to his ear, still watching Sabrina. And again he could not help but notice her legs, a fact which somehow amused him.

"Yes, Alec ?"

"Commander," Hobbs said, "there has been what could prove a very ugly development about the immigration problem."

"Yes ?" Gideon's voice sharpened as the door closed.

"Twenty-seven landlords, including Rataudi, and also including fourteen of those on his list, have received identical messages this morning, all posted at the same post office, the one behind the Strand, near Trafalgar Square, yesterday evening. In each case the message is unsigned, typewritten, and says: 'You shall hang by the neck until you are dead'."

Hobbs's voice, very precise and detached, seemed to give the phrase an extra touch of the macabre, as if the threat was simple earnest of what was to be. It repeated itself in his mind as he digested it: *You shall hang by the neck until you are dead.*

"What have you done about it so far?" asked Gideon.

"Arranged for each letter to be collected and brought here, and for each recipient to have a police guard, who . . ."

Behind Hobbs's voice, yet very clear and resonant and undoubtedly uttered to make sure he heard, came Rollo's voice saying: ". . . are going to give us a hell of a lot of trouble if we're not careful."

Hobbs did not stop, and showed no indication that he had heard the other man.

". . . will be visited every half hour by a patrol car."

"Don't see what else you can do," Gideon said. "But apparently Rollo has some thoughts on the matter. Send him in, will you? And listen in to us." There was a small amplifier on Hobbs's desk which could pick up anything said in Gideon's office provided he, Gideon, had switched on a microphone attached to his inter-office telephone.

"Thank you," Hobbs said.

There was no way of telling whether he left the receiver off deliberately or simply put it back loosely by accident; whichever it was, Gideon heard him say: "The Commander wishes to see you at once."

Gideon had a few seconds in which to decide on his attitude. Rollo was a good man with a first-class record of service covering nearly twenty years. He had a better-than-most record for physical courage, too. With both of these came an attitude which could at times be truculent and, occasionally, insubordinate. Handled well, he could be brilliant; handled badly, he could be obstructive and over-aggressive. There was no doubt at all that he had meant his words to carry, little doubt that Hobbs's icy manner had already served as a rebuke. But had it been effective? Or was Rollo making a play to get his own way?

CHAPTER 15

THE RENT COLLECTOR

ROLLO came in, almost breasting the door open, but he grabbed and stopped it before it slammed. He was obviously aware that he had created an atmosphere and was prepared to be bellicose about it.

Gideon was sitting down, very square in his chair.

"Sit down, Hugh," he said, and so set the pattern for his own mood and the next few moments. He contemplated the other's attractive face and greeny-grey eyes. The features were full, the lips very well-shaped. "I don't know how much the Deputy-Commander has told you," Gideon went on, "but I want a man who will work day and night on the investigation into what happened at Long Street, and also find out the actual strength of these opposing groups in our brand of the racial problem. It has to be someone who will keep his head under what could become extreme provocation, and who will keep in the closest touch — hour by hour if necessary — with me or Mr. Hobbs. No lone-wolfing. No treading on corns. His success or failure could mean a great deal, could actually avoid some open conflicts between racial groups." Gideon paused, while Rollo sat very square and upright in his chair; then he went on: "Until a few minutes ago I thought you were just such a man."

Rollo's face dropped, almost ludicrously, and as he began to recover, slowly, Gideon went on:

"If you've anything to report, complain about, join issue with, I want it straight. I don't want you or anyone else implying that someone else's handling of a job is lousy. I want it straight from you in the presence of the other man." He paused again, and when Rollo began to relax slightly but didn't speak, he demanded: "Is that understood?"

By now, Rollo was breathing deeply and there was no expression on his face except a curious kind of stubbornness.

"Yes, sir," he said.

"Good. What were you implying just now about the watch on these landlords?"

In a voice quite free from emotion and yet deep and quite captivating, Rollo answered: "It looks to me as if we've swung too far in protecting these people. I know they've their rights and we have to do what we can, but even some of the most reasonable people will soon start saying we're mollycoddling them, and yet we need public support." When Gideon didn't answer, Rollo went on: "If one side or the other gets the idea that we're prejudiced, then there'll be a hell of a lot of trouble. But no one here seems — *seemed* to realise it."

"We realise it," Gideon said flatly. He gave that time to sink in, and then added: "Any strong feelings either way?"

"On what?"

"On race."

"Not as far as I know," Rollo answered. He gave a fierce grin, showing that side of him which was probably the one women found so captivating. "Give me looks or intelligence, I don't care what they're packed in."

"Any anti-semitism in you?"

"No more than in most people. Nearly every non-Jew has a tinge of it," Rollo replied. "If you mean am I a Jew hater or a Jew-baiter, no. I'd break the neck of anyone who started any bloody nonsense."

"Could you work well with Piluski on this job?" asked Gideon.

Very quietly, most impressively, Rollo said: "There isn't a better detective on the Force and I'd be glad to work with him on any assignment. But it would be asking for trouble on this."

"Why?"

"The anti-colour fanatic is usually what Hitler called an Aryan, who believes in the pure Aryan blood and has a strong streak of anti-semitism. Piluski would be first-class if he could work on the job without running into prejudice from others — but he couldn't avoid running into it."

Gideon said: "I see."

"Don't you agree?" asked Rollo, and then in an almost defensive way, went on: "You did ask me for my opinion, didn't you?"

"Yes," Gideon said. "But there's another point of view."

"What is it?"

"If Piluski worked with you and couldn't

get co-operation from some of the people concerned, whereas you could, it would look as if they were prejudiced against him," said Gideon. "Then we'd know how to tackle them."

"That's a bit too devious," Rollo objected. "Don't you think so, sir?"

"I don't like the idea, here in London, of having to select a senior officer for an assignment because of his race or colour," Gideon said. After a pause, he went on: "Do you want to tackle this job?"

Rollo drew in a deep breath and then answered with great vehemence: "There is nothing I'd like more."

"Sharing responsibility with Piluski?"

"I'd accept your judgement about that," Rollo said.

"Right." Gideon nodded, and then switched to another aspect. "Do you know Saxby of AB Division well?"

"Not really well," answered Rollo. "But well enough, I think."

"Chief Inspector Archer?"

Rollo's face broke into the deep lines of another fierce grin.

"Now there's a man I could work hand-in-glove with! I was a C.I. when he got his promotion from detective officer to sergeant," Rollo went on. "We had about four years together out at NE Division before he was moved to AB and I was brought here and made a superintendent."

Gideon asked: "Were you quoting Archer just now?"

Rollo, a reply on the tip of his tongue before the question was framed, checked himself; then he said with a crooked smile: "I think he would agree with me; we mustn't show the slightest sign of being surprised at anything."

"All right," Gideon said drily. "How much did you work with Tom Riddell?"

"Not much, lately," answered Rollo. "Would that matter?"

"I wondered if he'd talked to you about what he's been doing, that's all," Gideon remarked, and placed a hand on the very thick file on his desk. "Here's his file. There'll be a lot more detail in his office. Go and look through it, will you? What we need most is information about potential terrorists on either side."

Rollo stood up, with obvious alacrity.

"Right away, sir."

"And when you think you're fully

briefed, come and see me again," Gideon ordered.

He gave Rollo his choice of door, and Rollo chose to go out through Hobb's office. The communicating door closed before Gideon could hear a word of what either man said. He himself rose and stood looking out into the Thames. He knew of at least one outstanding detective who did most of his thinking in his bath, another when eating alone, a third when on top of a London bus. For his part, most of his constructive thinking, both conscious and sub-conscious, was done when standing at this window and looking out at this scene which was so much the heart of London, watching the flowing Thames, lifeblood of the city. The sky was still leaden grey, the river itself hardly seemed to be moving. A police launch passed with its usual crew of three, one of the men standing in the stern holding his hooked pole. The launch was going slowly and its wash was sluggish.

Had the look-out seen something?

Gideon stayed for perhaps five minutes, thinking over all that Rollo had said, and also thinking about Piluski. After a while, he moved to the communicating door and opened it. Hobbs was in there alone, sitting at his desk. He began to get up.

"What was Rollo's reaction?" Gideon asked.

"He can hardly believe his luck," Hobbs reported, drily.

"And I think I'm going to assign Piluski to work with him," Gideon went on.

"The more I think about it the more I'm sure he's the right man," Hobbs conceded. "Rollo will drive ahead like a rocket, Piluski will make sure the ground's clean after him."

"What did you make of Rollo's argument?"

"In spite of all he says, he's nervous," answered Hobbs. "Practically everyone is where this race and immigration problem is involved. Somehow it forces them to play a kind of politics. Don't tell the truth, don't say what you think, for fear of offending someone or hurting their feelings or causing some kind of violent reaction. I think this is the job we can do that no one else can," went on Hobbs. "We don't have to show fear or favour. I don't think Rollo will, and I'm sure Piluski won't. But — " He hesitated as his exchange telephone bell rang, lifted it and covered the mouthpiece with his left hand, and went on: "I don't think we're going to be able to get quick results, Commander. We're going to have to play for time."

"That's what I'm afraid of," Gideon said. "All right, bring Piluski in as soon as he arrives, will you?"

He closed the door on Hobbs speaking into the telephone, and went back to his window stance. To his surprise, the police launch was still in sight; it appeared to have turned a full circle, and was still circling while the man with the boat-hook knelt on the edge, boat-hook poised in front of him. There was now no doubt at all that he had seen something in the water and was set on dragging it close for a better look. Suddenly, he leaned forward and a second member of the crew edged closer towards him. Gideon noticed a crowd gathered on the bridge and on the Embankment, spectators of a peep-show which was almost as exciting as a television drama.

There was a tap at the communicating door, Gideon turned round as it opened and Hobbs ushered Piluski in. Piluski came soft-footed. His thin face had a leathery look, so lined and grooved. His chin, very bony, seemed to curve out towards his nose. He had very thick lips, shaped remarkably like a harp, and his eyes were deep-set and so dark that it was almost impossible to doubt that he had lined them with eye-black. He was slight of build, small when standing against Hobbs, positively a pigmy by Gideon's side.

Gideon told him exactly what he wanted. Now and again Piluski interjected a question, first raising his right hand: the thumb and forefinger were dark-brown from incessant cigarette smoking; he held his cigarettes differently from most. Each question needed only a brief answer. The contrast between this man and Rollo was quite remarkable.

At last, Gideon finished: "We want anything — anything at all — to give us a sound case to make a criminal charge, from disturbing the peace to fraud."

"I understand perfectly." Piluski's voice was so deep that its gutteral tone was like a background noise and words were sometimes difficult to distinguish from one another.

"And of course we want the man or

men — women, for that matter — who sent these threats," Gideon said.

Piluski nodded.

"Will you take Polly along to see Rollo?" Gideon asked Hobbs.

Both the others stood up immediately, and as they went out Gideon dialled Riddell's office; Rollo answered, abruptly, on what must have been the first ring of the telephone.

"Rollo here."

"Mr. Hobbs is bringing Mr. Piluski along to your office," Gideon said. "You will be working together."

"Right, sir!" Rollo said briskly. "Thank you."

★　★　★

That was nearly half-past eleven, about the time when Carol Entwhistle got on to a train at Paddington Station. She had checked very carefully at the announcements board that she had to catch the next train from here, get off at Exeter and then catch a bus which would get her to Two Bridges, the nearest village to Dartmoor Prison, a fact she had read in a newspaper article. (She might have to change at

Princetown.) She would walk from the bus station. She had no idea what to do once she reached the prison, except to ask for her father.

She had no idea that it would be dark by the time she arrived.

She had no idea that, in November, thick fog was almost inevitable on the moor.

She had no idea that Horace Welbeck, serving a life sentence for the murder of an old woman whose house he had burgled, was planning to escape that night.

* * *

And that was the time, just after half-past eleven, when Ellen Wells stood at the window of the living-room and saw a policeman on the opposite side of the road; it was almost as if he were watching the house. She had thought yesterday that his interest had been in the couple upstairs and their jewellery, but surely that was over and done with. She was puzzled, and she was also deeply troubled by David's manner, but she had not yet connected the two. She went out into the garden to get in some washing which was already nearly dry. There was a spit of rain coming from skies which looked snow-laden. Then she saw tiny particles of powdered snow bouncing off the black wool of her jumper. Immediately her concern was for the children, who had not gone to school in their wellingtons but would need them if it snowed heavily. With the washing bundled up in her arms she hurried back to the house, but before she opened the back door one of David's socks fell off, near the dustbin. Rather than risk dropping the lot, she went inside and dumped the clothes on the kitchen table, then returned for the sock. Bending down for it, she saw the newspaper screwed up and torn, in the dustbin. She was puzzled — *she* hadn't thrown the *Morning Sun* away, and she couldn't believe that any of the children had. She checked the date; it was this morning's. She saw the front page, with its pictures of the dreadful disaster in Notting Hill. And she saw the inside page, with a photograph of a girl who had been strangled — no, suffocated — but she was never quite sure of the difference — not far away. Over the picture was the headline: *Police Have Clue to Girl's Murder*.

As she read the story, which was calculated to alarm the murderer but to give nothing away, she had an even stronger feeling that she was being watched. It made her go cold, and for a few moments she could not move. When at last she did, the policeman was staring at her over the garden fence.

She was to find out later that he was Police Constable Oswald.

She felt as if he were looking at her almost accusingly, but, something she could not have dreamed, in fact, it was in admiration. The feeling of interest in her as a woman faded when he crossed to the dustbin and saw the story which had been ripped across.

*   *   *

The story was in every newspaper.

Wherever David Wells looked, he seemed to see it. Even when he turned to give some typing to the girl behind him, there was a newspaper open at a full page picture of the girl he had murdered.

*   *   *

"You're young to be travelling alone, aren't you?" remarked the guard on the train as he clipped Carol's ticket.

"Yes, but you see I am going to visit my father," Carol Entwhistle explained, earnestly.

* * *

There was a noticeable change of mood in many parts of London, that day. The police noticed it, of course, although there was a possibility that they were so acutely aware of the situation that they almost imagined the mood. But the Press was acutely aware of it, too. It was especially noticeable in areas which had become almost exclusively coloured. There was truculence among the young, while little knots of women stood talking together and, a comparatively rare thing, Pakistanis and Jamaicans talked together. There was much anger and there was a great deal of resentment.

In a part of Fulham not far from the Lots Road Power Station, a little Pakistani named Munshi, Patel Munshi, was out on his daily rounds. He was a rent collector. His employer, a wealthy Pakistani, was not in fact a bad landlord and did not overcrowd his houses, although many who rented a room or two from him sub-let, and many rooms were too crowded. Munshi was, however, a loyal and painstaking employee, and whenever he saw indications of these abuses, he reported it; when essential plumbing and roof repairs was needed, he pushed for them to be done. He also pushed for the rent and was severe on anyone more than two weeks behind.

Bernard Oppenheimer Morris was now three weeks behind.

It was not his fault. A Jamaican who had been in England for three years, he was out of work. He didn't gamble, drink too much or spend money on women; in fact he was desperately worried about where he was going to get the money to feed his family. So when Munshi came for the rent of two rooms in a house where twenty people lived, he was already nervous and worried. Had he been apologetic, Munshi would doubtless have grumbled 'but agreed to wait for another week before reporting, but Bernard Oppenheimer was affected by the general mood.

"You can go and tell your boss he can sing for his money," he said in his deep and carrying voice.

"That is no way to talk to me, I will not permit it," protested Munshi.

"I damn well talk to you any way I wish to."

"I want your three weeks back-rent now and if you do not pay — " began Munshi.

He saw the Jamaican's hand spread out and felt it on his chest. He lost his balance, reeling backwards, and grabbed at Morris's wrist. He was oblivious of the crowd which had gathered in the street behind him, aware only of the big, hostile man in front of him. His skinny fingers clutched Morris's, but Morris pulled himself free without any effort, and then pushed again. Munshi went staggering backwards, missed the top step of four, and fell heavily.

As he fell, a long-haired, white youth kicked him in the ribs. Another white youth kicked him in the groin. A little Jamaican kicked at his shoulder, a Pakistani cried: "Do not kick him!" and the first white youth turned and kicked the protester, savagely. On the instant, a dozen people were fighting, and it was impossible to see who was kicking Munshi deliberately and who was kicking out at anyone in range, and who was simply trampling on him.

Munshi himself certainly didn't know; he was unconscious.

CHAPTER 16

SHORT TERM

AT twenty minutes to two, Rollo and Piluski left Gideon's office, where they had been for the past hour. Only Hobbs had stayed behind. The remains of a snack lunch sent from the canteen was on a table pushed into a corner, and the shadows of snowflakes made a shifting pattern in a silver-plated coffee-pot. Now, Gideon stood up and stretched, while Hobbs said:

"I can make notes of that in fifteen minutes, sir."

Gideon eyed him, without immediately speaking. Hobbs waited, obviously puzzled, as obviously aware that in spite of the intense concentration on the two reports from the widely different men in charge of the investigation now on file as *Long Street Incident*, his chief's attention had wandered. Gideon, in fact, had had the Commissioner hovering on his mind for some time, and now that he could relax from the actual task in hand, he had a vivid mental picture of Scott-Marle. The silence was prolonged more than he intended; long enough for Hobbs to show signs of strain.

"Alec," Gideon said at last. "Have you ever regretted joining the police?"

Hobb's expression changed, almost ludicrously; and before he answered he actually laughed.

"Not for a moment!"

"Quite the right way to spend your life?"

"Yes," Hobbs answered, and added shrewdly: "You must have a good reason for asking. Have I shown any sign of impatience or frustration lately?" When Gideon didn't answer he went on: "In a way, the longer I'm in the Force, the bigger the variety of problems we touch on, the more I feel involved. Get immersed in it, I mean. What *is* behind the question, George?"

Gideon moved suddenly, startlingly.

"I'll tell you later. Nothing that need disturb you, anyhow. Now you'd better get those notes down, I've got to be in Scott-Marle's office in fifteen minutes."

Hobbs went out, taking his own notebook with him, and Gideon went across to his desk and sat on the corner as he dialled *Information*. The moment he was answered, he said:

"Gideon. What is the latest report on the rent collector Munshi?"

"On the danger list, sir — not doing well."

"Hmm. And on Superintendent Riddell?"

"Very satisfactory, sir."

"Good," Gideon said. "I shall be in the Commissioner's office at two o'clock, if there is any further news on the man Munshi, call me there."

"Very good, sir."

Gideon sifted through all of his files again, only too well aware that whenever there was a case which demanded extra concentration it brought a danger of overlooking something of importance in other cases. The two which made him pause were the post office robbery and the Entwhistle investigation. All the indications in the main robbery showed that it had been carried out with great verve, with all the daring of an "amateur" coup. Not a single fingerprint, not a single clue, had yet been discovered. He pushed this file aside, and considered the latest report from Honiwell. It was wholly to do with Eric Greenwood, and included the fact that, according to his secretary, he was planning to go to India for several weeks.

Could that mean that he was beginning to realise that he was under suspicion?

And should he be allowed to go?

There was a note from Honiwell. "We might be advised to take some step before he leaves the country." Yes, thought Gideon, we might indeed. Perhaps he, Gideon, needed some such prompting to prevent him from sitting on the fence. He took a quick look at the report from Ealing on the Rosamund Lee murder. They seemed very sure of themselves and Wilson wasn't a man to jump to conclusions. There was a note that the man under surveillance was married with three children all between five and nine. If he had killed the girl, why? The usual motive: his wife might find out about his peccadillo?

Peccadillo, Gideon thought. Light word for what could be one of the most tragic situations in society. How many married men, at this moment, were having an *affaire* outside their marriage? How many were fearful of the wife finding out? How many other women were desperately unhappy, wanting the man to get a divorce? How many men were tempted to kill? "If only she would die." What was wrong? The society, the conventions, and the religious teaching, which made both men and women believe that extra-marital sex was wrong, even in this so-called permissive age? There was as much ache and pain as ever when a marriage was threatened. Or were the conventions, the Ten Commandments, right? Thou shalt not steal . . . thou shalt not kill . . . thou shalt not covet thy neighbour's wife . . . thou shalt not commit adultery . . . Were these Commandments the right injunctions to man? Was man himself too frail a creature to observe them? Or were they indeed Commandments which no man could be expected to keep? What would society be like if there had never been the Ten Commandments?

There was a light tap on the communicating door and Hobbs appeared.

Gideon, looking at his watch, saw that it was two minutes to two.

"Any particular problem?" he asked.

"I think the leads of several different aspects are there," said Hobbs. "And yet — "

"Yes?"

"I've a sense that something's missing," stated Hobbs.

"Missing," echoed Gideon. "I'll have a look. Thanks."

What did Hobbs mean? he asked himself. Missing, missing, missing. This was Hobb's strength: a kind of sixth sense which made him uneasy when he did not feel he could see everything there was to see about a case. Gideon had this same sixth sense; as if an antenna was jutting out and receiving a signal but the message wasn't understood. As he walked along towards the lift, he scanned the notes, written in a clear hand with the headings in block capitals. There was the whole story of what had happened, concisely stated. Obviously much of this had been written before Hobbs had seen Rollo and Piluski. *Was* there something missing? There were date, time, place, damage, injuries, dead, with all details, number of people evacuated from the block before it had collapsed, *eleven hundred and three.* In eleven houses . . .

What a wicked thing it was!

How much responsibility did Rataudi have?

There was another heading: *Criminal charge considered: Manslaughter.* That was about it. There were the civil offences against local byelaws, and London County Council regulations. He read on, to the activity of the police, the number of landlords protected, the number actually attacked. Details of the actual crimes were here: the attempt to break into houses, uttering menaces and, finally, the vicious attack on the little rent collector, Munshi.

Gideon reached Scott-Marle's door.

What *had* Hobbs meant? And was there really something missing, or was there simply a sense of frustration, that there was so little the police could do? Gideon went into the outer room where Scott-Marle's secretary usually sat: and Sabrina Sale looked up from the secretary's desk.

"Why, hallo," Gideon said.

"Good afternoon, Commander," responded Sabrina, primly. "The Commissioner is expecting you, please go straight in."

"How is it you're here?" asked Gideon.

"I don't really know," Sabrina Sale answered, "but there's a lot of flu about." She gave her nice, wicked smile. "I have to keep everyone at bay while you're with the Commissioner. But all your letters are done, Commander. I'll have them sent to your office."

"Good," Gideon said appreciatively.

He didn't exactly forget Sabrina as he tapped on the door of Scott-Marle's office and went in; in fact he reached the point of thinking if she impressed Scott-Marle with her efficiency as much as she did him, then she might find herself the Commissioner's secretary, and he felt a slight, a very slight pang. Then he saw Scott-Marle behind his large, pedestal desk, almost bare of papers, in the rather big and sparsely-furnished room: and he saw Sir Thomas Bartlett, Permanent Under Secretary at the Home Office.

He now had not the slightest doubt of the seriousness with which the situation was regarded. Bartlett was the senior civil servant at the Home Office and was known to have a great deal of influence with a succession of Home Secretaries, who themselves had influence with the Cabinet and, indeed, the Prime Minister. He wore a well-tailored black jacket, striped trousers and silver-grey tie.

He stood up, to shake hands.

"Nice to see you again, Commander."

"And to see you, sir."

"Good afternoon, Commander," Scott-Marle said. "Sit down."

Gideon pulled up a chair. "Thank you, sir." As he sat down he saw Bartlett hitch his chair round and had an immediate sense that these two had been in conference for some time and had perhaps lunched together; probably they had agreed that the civil servant should speak first. Gideon knew Bartlett as a formal man who had a great regard for the conventions and tradition, also as a man who always sought a precedent before taking any action; yet he could, in emergency, slash red tape. He could be off-putting, often seeming to think of something else when talking, but there was no doubt now of his degree of concentration.

"Commander," he said, "there is grave anxiety at the highest level about what happened yesterday and its possible consequences."

"That's good," said Gideon, obviously to Bartlett's surprise.

"I don't quite — oh. I see. You were afraid it would not be taken seriously enough."

"I hoped it wouldn't be considered a police matter only, sir." As he spoke, Gideon knew that in a way he was fencing: and then quite suddenly, almost as if they had been flashed into his mind by some outside force, he saw not one but *two* things which neither he nor Hobbs had yet seen. First: that this was a police matter if any of the people in the collapsed houses had been illegal immigrants; second, that it was possible that the collapse had not been due simply to overcrowding and the weakening of foundations and wall-supports so as to make more room. Some of the foundations might have been weakened deliberately to induce a collapse.

Inwardly, he was seething at his own temporary blindness; and at the same time, excited and overpoweringly anxious to check this second possibility. Outwardly, he sat as impassive as Scott-Marle.

"These are police matters," Bartlett said.

"Indeed they are," said Scott-Marle.

"I think I've covered them all," said Gideon, but he did not take out Hobbs's notes; the omissions were too glaring. "But the basic cause of the trouble, the collapse, seems to be the primary concern of the Ministry of Housing and the local authority." He still felt that in a way he was fencing, and now that his mind was open to the possibility of sabotage, it was as if floodgates had opened to allow ideas to stream in. "We can find out how many of the people who lived there were illegal immigrants, of course, and came in excess of the quota from any country concerned, but that's going to take a long time, and might best be handled by the immigration authorities."

"Why not the police?" demanded Bartlett.

"Because we don't want the police to become the whipping boys," answered

Gideon. "We are going to have a great deal of investigation to do, we want the utmost co-operation from the legal and illegal immigrants, but if at the same time we are the spearhead of the attack to find out who's been smuggled in, then a great number simply aren't going to talk." He shot a glance at Scott-Marle as he went on: "I've discussed one aspect of this from time to time, sir, with successive Assistant Commissioners: the need for both West Indian and Pakistani policemen and Criminal Investigation Department officers. Often these will be able to communicate with immigrant population more effectively than English-born-and-bred officers. A great number of immigrants are scared of us because they can't understand us."

Scott-Marle said: "We've put this to you often, Sir Thomas."

"And we've placed it before those in authority," Bartlett answered.

"Like nearly everything to do with this problem its been put off and put off," Gideon said, "and I'm as guilty as the next man. But we can't — no one can — afford to procrastinate any further."

Bartlett, who had rather a vague expression and features, suddenly became surprisingly forceful. "And we most certainly will not," he said.

"I'm very glad to hear it, sir." When no one made further comment, he went on: "But I imagine you want more from me than a declaration of principles!" He settled back in his chair. "Every practical precaution against reprisals has been taken, but after the attack on the rent collector this morning the situation is even more delicate. If he should die — " He broke off.

"What do your reports from the Divisions say?" asked Scott-Marle.

"That there is a great deal of restlessness and resentment," said Gideon, "and some indication that extreme anti-immigrationists are ready to move in."

"Move in?" echoed Bartlett, sharply.

"As they moved in where the rent collector was concerned. None of our men was present but we've had full reports. That began as an incident between immigrants — a tenant and a rent collector. We've made no arrests although the tenant appears to have started the trouble.

White youths went in and made it far worse. They obviously plan to create a serious disturbance. They want the trouble to appear to be inherent in immigration. All we can do where that is concerned is watch, protect, and investigate. Instructions have gone out to the Divisions to this effect, gentlemen. And I've assigned two senior officers, Superintendents Rollo and Piluski, to the case and have given them authority to use as many junior officers as they need. I've talked to *Uniform* and I've sent a teletype message to the Divisions calling for this investigation to be given priority."

Scott-Marle said: "Good."

"Do you have enough men to do this properly?" asked Bartlett.

"In the short term, yes. In the long term, no."

"I have no doubt that the Commander will shortly point out that this is another job we can't do properly because we're under strength," Scott-Marle said drily.

"I will most certainly point it out to those in authority," promised Bartlett. "Has your team discovered anything that hasn't been reported, Commander?"

Gideon said: "No. They have had very little time since the disaster. However — " He paused, and both men showed immediate interest; waited on his words. "There is one possibility we need help with, sir — Fire Service help, perhaps the bomb-disposal, and also construction engineers."

"What are you driving at? demanded Scott-Marle.

"That collapse was remarkably uniform," Gideon pointed out, giving thanks that he had thought of this in time. "They are old Victorian houses which were very solidly built, yet they collapsed almost like a pack of cards. It may have been because the main support walls and pillars had been weakened to make sleeping alcoves, but it's conceivable that the foundations were deliberately weakened by fanatical anti-blacks, so that once a collapse started, the whole block would come down. This would not only kill a lot of immigrants, but draw attention to the overcrowding, the take-over of whole districts, as the fanatics say."

He saw the alarm on the faces of the

others; on men well-trained not to show their emotions. They had been hanging on his words before, but now additional tension had come into this room.

And it came to him, and he was suddenly fearful and afraid.

Just as he had realised what was missing soon after Hobbs had drawn attention to the fact that something was, now that he had been talking, the full logical consequence of this possibility struck him. He sensed that it had already begun to occur to the others as he went on:

"And if it was sabotage, it might not be confined to the one place. Other blocks might already have been weakened — it would be easy enough, a few bricks at a time. Other collapses might well come." He went on in a grim voice, as if he had been deliberately leading up to this harsh climax. "And Black Power extremists might conceivably create such a situation so as to draw attention to the shocking conditions." He paused for a moment before going on: "The certain thing is, gentlemen, that we mustn't take any chances. We have to find out, now. We have to have every block of overcrowded houses inspected for sabotage in a matter of days. In fact, if I had my way it would be done today."

CHAPTER 17

SEARCH IN LONDON

THERE was utter silence in the office when Gideon finished, silence which seemed to last a long time although in fact it was less than a minute. Gideon felt the gaze from each of the others, wondered for a few moments whether they thought him exaggerating, and then saw Bartlett shift in his seat.

"How many such places are there, Commander?"

"Certainly not less than thirty," Gideon answered.

"Can you provide a list quickly? — without going through the local authorities, I mean."

"Yes," Gideon said. "We can supply that thirty and get the other places checked for attention after the thirty have been done."

Bartlett glanced at Scott-Marle.

"Can you make arrangements with bomb-disposal?"

"Yes. At once."

"Then I will start things moving with the mining engineers," said Bartlett. "Do you have any ideas as to how to set about it, Commander?"

"Yes," Gideon answered in turn. "I'll have Divisional men at all the suspect places within a quarter of an hour. If you'll have the engineers contact me, I'll tell them where to go. And I'll have our Map Room prepare a map for a Report Centre. We can use *Information* at a pinch but I'd rather Rollo and Piluski kept their finger on the situation."

"I will proceed at once," Bartlett promised. Then he paused and looked at Scott-Marle with a faint smile, hesitated for a few moments and added: "The other matter can wait, Commissioner, but I think I shall agree with you. If you will excuse me — "

Quick as he was, Scott-Marle beat him to the door, obviously wanting Gideon to stay. Sabrina Sale was talking on the telephone in a polite but insistent way. The door shut out her voice and cut Bartlett off from sight. Scott-Marle stood by Gideon, leaning against his desk.

"Do you have any evidence of sabotage to go on, George?"

"No," Gideon said. "I only glimpsed the possibility just before I told you."

Scott-Marle replied drily: "You saw the other possibility, no doubt."

"That this way we can check on all the cases of over-crowding quickly," Gideon agreed. "And without creating a lot of problems." He grinned broadly. "If they think their house might fall down on them, they'll co-operate! We should be able to get a report for the Home Office in forty-eight hours instead of taking a couple of months." The more he saw of the consequences of that discovery of the "missing" factors, the more it pleased him. "I must get moving, sir."

"Yes. George — "

"Sir?"

"I am more than ever sure that you should be the Assistant Commissioner," said Scott-Marle. "That was what Sir Thomas and I were going to discuss with you. We had agreed over lunch that whatever you say, you are our man. And Donaldson isn't coming back at all," Scott-Marle added. "The appointment has to be made soon, and it is absurd for you to be doing the job and doubling it with that of the Commander. You do see that, don't you?"

Gideon said heavily: "Yes, sir, I see it."

He saw other things, too. First that he must concentrate on the raids; second, that his reaction to this Assistant Commissionership was unchanged; he did not want the job, and certainly he did not want to be pushed into it. Scott-Marle didn't force the issue any further but opened the door for him. Sabrina had a sheet of paper in her typewriter, and was typing fast. Gideon glanced at her and she smiled up, obviously preoccupied. He went out and strode along the passages, along comparatively unfamiliar passages, for the Commissioner was housed in a different part of the building. There was a short cut, using a back lift to Riddell's old office, and he reached it as Piluski was arriving from the other direction. Piluski opened the door.

Inside, one wall was already covered with a map of the Greater London area, an enlargement of the one in Riddell's file. Three detective officers, including a detective sergeant from the Map Room, were filling in the concentrated areas with red-headed pins. Four other men were seated at a long trestle-table, each with a telephone in front of him. Two engineers were fitting in a teletype machine. In the middle of all this, Rollo was sitting at a desk which was much too small for him, brooding over some reports, while a man near by was banging away on a typewriter, as if utterly oblivious of what was going on about him.

"Hugh," Piluski said, and Rollo put his left hand up, palm outwards, while he read a page of a report. Then he glanced up, saw Gideon, started back and sprang to his feet.

"Sorry, sir."

"All right," Gideon said. "We've got that reason for getting into every place which might be overcrowded. The reason: yesterday's collapse could have been due partly to sabotage. I want to talk to the Royal Army Ordnance Corps, and you'll find out what we have to do as I talk."

The R.A.O.C. was at first startled, then almost instantly understanding and eager to co-operate with a team to help search the houses.

As he finished and the full possibilities

struck home, Rollo said: "My God!" and Piluski placed the tips of his fingers together, rather as Rataudi had done, as if he were praying for guidance.

Gideon went on, sharply and to the point, until all of them there knew what they were expected to do, and he finished: "You're halfway on with the job already."

"Intelligent anticipation," Rollo said. "We'll co-operate with everyone, don't worry, sir. We'll have a man to liaise with the engineers."

"That I shall look after," Piluski said, happily.

Gideon, completely satisfied by the way these two men were tackling their job, went out at once. He walked straight into Hobbs's office, where Hobbs stood up from his desk, set slant-wise across a corner so that he could get the best light from the window. As Gideon told him what he had arranged, snow fell very heavily outside, and he reflected that there was going to be a bad night in which to operate. Now and again Hobbs nodded; once, he shook his head as if in bewilderment.

"And you haven't been away an hour," he observed.

"Your 'something missing' was the clue," Gideon said.

He relaxed for the first time since he had started from here for Scott-Marle's office, with a glow of well-being and a hint of physical reaction. He was *tired*. There was truth in Scott-Marle's argument that he couldn't continue to do both jobs, but his reaction was still the same. *His* job was that of Commander. He wanted to be in constant touch with the men out in the field. He did not want to be an administrator. And he could serve the Yard much more effectively as Commander than as Assistant Commissioner. Take today, for instance: who else could have had the background knowledge of the men available ? Who else could have known instinctively that Piluski was the right man to work with Rollo, and have the satisfaction of knowing, so quickly that no one at the Yard was better equipped than Piluski to liaise with the engineers and the Bomb Disposal units they would send along ?

As these thoughts were passing through his mind, Hobbs was watching him. Hobbs. There was the man for Scott-Marle. This possibility had been in and out of his mind several times. Hobbs was exactly the right man. Young enough to serve ten or even fifteen years as Assistant Commissioner. Young enough to serve as A.C. until Scott-Marle was ready to retire, and then to take over even that job. As these thoughts ran into his mind he was more sure than ever that he was right.

Hobbs's expression suggested that he knew that some fresh and invigorating idea was passing through Gideon's mind, but caution warned Gideon: no matter how sure he felt now he had to sleep on it, had to check from every angle. And there was more than enough to do today, already.

It was half-past four, and the whole of the campaign was under way. It was like a military operation with the field head-quarters in Riddell's office. There was irony in the fact that Riddell lay in his hospital bed, his wife by his side, while the work he had started had flared into tremendous activity. When his telephone bell rang he plucked it up, almost exasper-ated because it had to break his train of thought.

"Commander." It was Honiwell, and all irritation faded. "I thought you should

know this at once. The child Carol Entwhistle didn't go to school today: she
played truant. I've only just heard from her
aunt, who is terrified in case Carol's gone
to Dartmoor to try to see her father."

* * *

Carol was only a little over ten years old.

She looked in some ways older than her
years, and no one questioned her when she
left the train at Exeter and went to catch
the bus she was told would go to Dartmoor.
By the time she reached the place, at four
o'clock, it was already dark and misty, and
there were few lights and few people about.

She began to feel scared, but the urgent
and irresistible desire to see her father kept
her going. She sensed that if she asked for
the prison she would be asked why she
wanted to go there; she had to find the
gates by herself. The great high walls, the
tops actually hidden by the fog, seemed
harsh and bleak, but somewhere behind
them was her father.

* * *

"Entwhistle," a warder said, in the library.
"What is it?" Entwhistle asked.

"Have you seen Welbeck this after-noon?"

"No, sir," Entwhistle said. The "sir" demanded a great effort, and his body went tense, his fingers crooked. How he hated these men! How he would love to choke the life out of them.

The warder had a harsh voice and a hard manner. He stood close to Entwhistle who was in the library; only a few other prisoners were there, selecting books. The warder kept his voice low, so that it did not carry, and he had the sense to realise how close to revolt this prisoner was.

"You wouldn't lie to me, would you?"

Somehow, Entwhistle maintained his self-control. He had to, he had to, but how he would like to choke the life out of this man! All the calmness of despair which had once soothed him had gone.

"Why the hell should I?" His voice rose.

"Be careful how you talk to me," the warder warned. Then he asked a question which made Entwhistle understand some-thing of what was driving him. Welbeck, a trusty who acted as messenger between warders, did odds and ends of jobs in-cluding cleaning the library, was in for "life" because of a now ten-year-old murder. Like all trusties, he was taken for granted, and not noticed until he was wanted. "Are you sure you haven't seen him since luncheon?"

Entwhistle asked sharply: "What's the matter? Has he escaped?"

"Keep your voice low," the warder whispered savagely. "If you see him, report to me at once."

Entwhistle no longer had any doubt that Welbeck was missing. He himself had a sudden revulsion of feeling. What a night to be out on the moor! The few glimpses he could get of the yard, from the library windows, showed how thick and eerie the fog was inside four walls. Outside, the whole village must be shrouded, and not far from the prison walls there were the quarries and the open moorland, the wet grass and moss and peat, the patches of marshland, here and there the patches of bog. It was a night when the chances of being caught were negligible, but the chances of getting far from the prison were even smaller.

Entwhistle, with another revulsion of feeling, felt savage envy.

If only *he* could summon up the courage to escape . . .

One day, of course, he would, and he wouldn't be caught and allow himself to come back here: he would kill himself first. There was no hope from the police: that bloody parson had raised his hopes only to dash them; that plaster saint Gideon didn't care a damn. He, Entwhistle, would never see his children again until they were grown up, strangers. Better never to see them than through the prison grille.

As these things coursed searingly through his mind, the warder who had spoken to him reported to the chief warder on the block. He did this quietly, so as not to arouse unnecessary alarm, for Welbeck might be somewhere in the prison, hiding, or even dozing. Word was sent to the Assistant Governor, then to the Governor himself. A search of the prison was put in hand during the evening meal, but there was no sign of the trusty, and at last the message was flashed to the prison authorities and to the police not only of Dartmoor and Devon, but everywhere.

And the alarm siren went, high-pitched and frightening in the fog-laden night.

Searchlights were turned on, but the fog only reflected the glare and did no good at all.

*　*　*

Carol's heart leapt wildly when she first heard the wail of the siren; and as it rose, the fog about her seemed to become bright, as if an unearthly light had appeared from the hidden skies. Her heart pounded as she had never known before; the light on the swirling grey fog almost blinded her. She was close to a low brick wall, ankle deep in wet grass.

Her whole body shook.

Her heart seemed actually to lift in her chest and rise and choke her; and it reverberated through her whole body.

The wailing went on and on and on; the light seemed to grow brighter.

Suddenly, she heard voices.

Then, she heard the panting breath of a dog or man.

Some way off, she saw a tiny circle of misted light, like a halo held at a man's waist. It moved and waved about in little circles. The voices, close by for a few moments, went further away. She could still hear the panting of the creature, but not so close.

She tried to shout, but could not. The awful lump in her throat hurt so much and kept every sound back. She gasped for breath. The halo of light disappeared, and the noises faded. She realised, as her terror subsided, that the wailing had stopped. Slowly, very slowly, the pounding of her heart stopped, also, but she began to shiver. Head to foot, arms and legs, the shivering possessed her. She was not old enough to know that it was reaction from the fright, and that cold made it worse. It just possessed her; her head bobbed up and down and her teeth chattered as she shook.

Sounds died away, but the fog remained aglow.

The fog so enshrouded her that she could not see the squares of light at a row of cottages less than fifty yards away. There was no way of telling that the stone wall against which she huddled was the wall of a cottage garden, that safety and warmth were so close to her.

After a long time, her shivering eased. She was still very cold and a spasm shook her from time to time, but she was no longer gripped with ague. She straightened up. She began to beat her breast, flinging her arms about her as she had often seen Clive do when he was cold. And she could almost hear her aunt, saying: "Of course you'll be cold if you just stand there. Jump about, walk, run — you'll soon warm yourself up."

So, she began to walk, beating her arms about her as she went.

She could not run because the ground was so uneven, but gradually she walked more quickly, and suddenly she came upon a path. It was rough and there were loose stones, but it was a path and it must lead somewhere. More quickly than ever, she began to walk away from the village.

* * *

Welbeck was a mile away now, both blessing and cursing the fog, which had enabled him to climb a wall unseen. Somewhere at the end of a copse of trees a few yards off the main road there was a motor-cycle, tank filled with petrol, all ready to go. He had only to find it to have a real chance.

The wailing had stopped, but the warders

and the dogs were out and if he stayed free long enough, the soldiers would join the hunt, too. Probably the road blocks were going up already. That was the first thing the police did. For they would know he was as far away from the actual prison as he could be, so there was no point in staying near; that way he would have no hope in the morning. They would block the roads and search all traffic. They would know that any seasoned Dartmoor prisoner would keep as close to the roads as he could, for these were his life-lines. As they drew further from the village and the prison themselves, these roads drew further apart and the moorland was full of death-traps even for a grown man.

Every now and again Welbeck, a big man with huge hands and feet, saw the glow of headlights in the fog. To some, this would have had a glow of ethereal radiance; to him, it was simply confirmation that he was close to a road and not in great danger. It would be better to go back to that hell of a prison than to die.

He hadn't given up hope, yet; he had only just started.

But my God — what a night! He was

already cold through and through and his heavy boots, built for working on the moors felt damp and icy, too.

Once he crossed a path, his footsteps ringing out, and he froze to stillness in case he had been heard.

Only silence came, and the swirling fog.

CHAPTER 18
SEARCH ON DARTMOOR

THE Governor of Dartmoor was with his chief warder. He looked a little like Scott-Marle, but was younger and his hair was jet-black. He was a good administrator, in many ways, but just now extremely worried, so he had a tendency to ask superfluous questions.

"Is every cell checked?" he wanted to know.

"Every cell and every corner. He's over the wall, sir, no doubt about that."

The chief warder was a chunky man with a massive chin, and hair growing low over his forehead: almost simian in appearance. His hard life dealing with some of Britain's toughest criminals had not turned him into a brute.

"Are the road blocks up?" asked the Governor.

"Yes, sir. The police co-operated very quickly, as always."

"Good. What about military aid?"

"We could do with it, sir — miracles

can happen on a night like this. I should apply, sir."

"I will. Did Welbeck have outside help, do you think?"

"There's no evidence of it, sir."

"What do you think of his chances?" asked the Governor, anxiously.

"Unless he does have outside help, not a chance in a thousand," answered the chief warder. "It's been a very wet autumn and the marshes and bogs are at their worst. There's been a round-up of ponies to keep them off dangerous areas. But Welbeck's a cunning old bastard — begging your pardon, sir. He'll have gone from here like a shot from a bow, but he'll keep close to the roads. The police are in full agreement about that. We're concentrating on all roads and paths a mile or more away from the prison. *I* think we could start two or even three miles away, but their way is probably safer."

"I would think so," agreed the Governor. "If we find the slightest clue, let me know."

"Yes, sir," the chief warder promised.

He was reflecting that there was one particularly good thing about this Governor:

he didn't waste a lot of time in recrimination. There would be an investigation into Welbeck's escape, and disciplinary action if the inquiry showed anyone to blame, but the job in hand was to find Welbeck. He hesitated in front of the big square desk.

"Is there something else?" the Governor asked.

"Yes and no, sir. I'm sorry to be vague. Entwhistle *could* be involved."

"Entwhistle," the Governor echoed, and there was a softening in his expression. "How?"

"Welbeck was often in the library, sir. They saw a lot of each other. And when he was questioned, Entwhistle was obviously very much on edge. It's just possible that he knows how and when Welbeck escaped, but when he was being questioned he gave the impression that he might go berserk."

The Governor sat up very straight, and looked excessively severe.

"Will it help us find Welbeck if we know how and when he escaped?"

"Not tonight, sir," the chief warder said. "There's another thing, too, sir." When the Governor nodded, he went on:

"One of Entwhistle's children, a ten-year-old girl, ran away from home this morning, and was seen at Exeter this afternoon. Her train was an hour late at St. David's station. No one saw her after that."

For a few moments the Governor simply stared at him, but at last he said:

"Think she's heading for the prison?"

"It could be sir. I've asked our chaps to look out for her, just in case she's around. The police are on the look-out for her, too."

"Poor little devil," said the Governor, then added comfortably: "But she's probably all right. Where is Entwhistle?"

"In his cell, sir."

"Have a special watch kept on him, and keep me closely informed," ordered the Governor, and nodded dismissal.

The chief warder went off to help to organise and supervise the search on Dartmoor. He did not believe that Welbeck would have a chance to get far away unless he had already broken through the natural defences of the prison. He did believe that there had been some slackness, some carelessness, even conceivably some co-operation with the escaped killer, either by other

276

trusties, such as Entwhistle, or by an employee. He, the chief warder, would carry the brunt of responsibility, and the best hope of easing the burden was to re-capture Welbeck.

By now, the moor was alive with police and warders, and the military would soon join them. It was like beating the bounds; or a hunt, with a man as the quarry. The whole of the moor was under surveillance and there was an ever-widening circle. He, the chief warder, felt it more likely that Welbeck was a long way from the prison itself, and there was no point in searching the village or the prison yards.

And within the area he was sure was clear, Carol went walking, stumbling, terrified, cold; and very hungry.

* * *

The first reports about the damage at Long Street to reach the office at the Yard where Rollo and Piluski were in charge, were both good and bad.

There was no sign of sabotage; but there were some reports of hideous overcrowding. Rollo was out in an area near Islington, in North London. Piluski was across the river in a smaller area in Battersea. Gideon, thought of going home forgotten, was at his desk when there was a tap at the passage door, and Honiwell came in. He looked brisk and alert, and his appearance had changed a little because he had had a haircut some time during the day.

"Any word of that child?" Gideon asked. "Sit down."

"Yes," Honiwell said. "Exeter police found a ticket collector who saw her on the 11.30 train to Exeter this morning. He identified her photograph at once."

"Have you talked to Devon?" asked Gideon.

"Yes, sir; as you were deeply involved in this other business, I talked to Chief Superintendent Biddlecome at Exeter. He's alerted all his patrols, and will get in touch if there's any news, but his forces are stretched pretty thin. Did you hear about the escape?"

Gideon sat back in his chair as Honiwell at last began to sit down. He felt as if he had been slapped across the face, and did not speak for a few moments. At last, he said:

"From Dartmoor?"

"Yes. There's a full-scale search under way."

"So there should be a better chance of finding the child," Gideon observed, hopefully. He began to smooth the bowl of his pipe, looking at Honiwell as if he were trying to see into his mind. "The prisoners have television in their recreation room, don't they?"

"Yes, sir."

"Is there any risk of Carol's journey being reported on television or in the newspapers?" Gideon was thinking that if Entwhistle knew that his daughter might be lost on the moor it could snap the thin thread of self-control and cause a flood of temporary insanity.

"As far as I know, no one's found out. The aunt certainly won't talk. I did wonder, sir — " Honiwell broke off.

"Go on."

"Whether this might be a chance for me to go and see Entwhistle. To go and see him and tell him about his daughter and at the same time, tell him that we are making inquiries." Honiwell raised his hands breast high. "He must be feeling like hell. And if he hears about his daughter without some

279

compensating good news he might lose his mental balance. It's been touch and go with him for weeks, I'm told."

Gideon, who had been thinking hard as the other talked, said slowly: "Yes. Yes, I think you ought to go down in the morning. But not until morning. Let me know the latest before you go."

Honiwell looked both relieved and grateful.

"I will, sir. Thank you. Er — anything from the big search yet?"

"Nothing conclusive," Gideon replied. "Except that the overcrowding in some places is as bad if not worse than it was at Long Street." He nodded, and Honiwell went out slowly and deliberately. He stood up and went to the window and looked out on to a beautifully misty night, not foggy, just misty with the colour of pearls. There were the three-lamp standards over the bridge with wide haloes and the lights on the Embankment each held a halo, too. The moving beams from cars made the mist seem like ectoplasm; ghostly, thought Gideon, and he wasn't being fanciful. There were lights at the County Hall reflecting, like the bridge lamps, on the smooth surface of the water. It reminded him that he did not know whether that Thames Division patrol boat had found anything in the river. And it reminded him, as he was so often reminded, of the unsuspected crime which was undoubtedly taking place throughout London at that very moment, the crimes being planned, of which the police would know nothing until the morning: perhaps for days, or even weeks.

His Yard exchange telephone bell rang; he recognised the tone of the ringing, and went across to it.

"Gideon."

Piluski's throaty voice set the ear-piece quivering.

"Piluski here, sir," he said. "I think you would be advised to come and see the place I am in now." After a pause, he went on: "It has to be seen to be believed. I think we would be well-advised to have both Press and television on coverage, too."

"Where are you?" Gideon asked. "Still in Battersea?"

"Yes, sir. Pentecost Street."

Gideon almost groaned at the name.

As Gideon was driven across Battersea Bridge, where the smoke from the great Power Station chimneys looked sulphurous and hazed with red from neon lighting caught and carried by the mist, three things of direct concern to him were happening in London.

David Wells was riding his bicycle along a poorly-lit street, away from his home. He had to get rid of it quickly. The evening papers had mentioned a bicycle clue, and he had lost his head. He *had* to get rid of it and the quickest way was to push it into the river somewhere off Chiswick Steps. He had removed all traces of his ownership, as far as he could tell, wiped the front mud-guard, handlebars, frame, bell, brake levers, everything. He would not be able to rest until the cycle was gone. His panic was such that he had not thought of what questions would be asked because the bicycle was missing.

What he did not know was that a police-man had been watching him; and that the policeman, Oswald, could hardly wait for him to pass before pulling out his radio, and to report the moment he was answered:

"It's the same man, sergeant — the one

I saw the night before last. I'm positive. The light's about the same, too. I'd know if it was someone else."

"Good," the sergeant said. "We'll have him tailed for a bit longer, see what he's up to."

* * *

"Why has he gone out so soon after supper?" Ellen Wells asked herself, hopelessly.

Had he gone to see *her*? Whoever she was.

And then she added, aloud: "Will he come back?"

* * *

At the same moment a little man known to be a runner for antique and picture shops, telephoned the NE Divisional Superintendent, Lemaitre, at his home.

"I can tell you where Max is," the informer said. "But I need fifty quid, Mr. Lemaitre. Can you go to fifty quid?"

* * *

Detective Sergeant Benbow entered a small restaurant in Fulham Road, and was met by a young Cockney who led him down-stairs into converted cellars which made it much more spacious than it had seemed to be from the outside. This was an English food restaurant where every variety of home cooking was a speciality, from Yorkshire pudding with gravy to steak and kidney pies and puddings, Lancashire hot-pot, roast beef, stuffed loin of lamb and stuffed shoulder of veal, black sausage and faggots, sausage and mash and toad-in-the-hole — luscious pork sausages cooked in a batter. Practically every traditional dish was available, and this restaurant had been here under the same ownership for seven years.

The wife of the partnership was both the *madame* at the desk and the "wine" waiter; but here only British beers and ales and stouts were served, with elderberry and ginger wines made from the berries of the hedgerows of England as well as ciders and English gin and whisky, the only spirits available. Benbow settled in a corner with a table beneath which he could stretch his legs. The big, handwritten menu did him a world of good, and when the woman came to inquire what he would drink, he had already decided on Devonshire cider.

As she nodded approval, he drew out Greenwood's photograph and showed it to her.

"Well, fancy seeing Mr. Greenwood again!" she exclaimed, without a moment's hesitation. "I often wondered why he stopped coming. He came here regularly once, always had the same girlfriend with him, a really lovely young woman. She — "

Benbow took out a photograph of Margaret Entwhistle and placed it by the side of Greenwood's picture.

"Love-a-duck!" exclaimed the woman. "That's the woman!"

She had a remarkably good memory, and she talked freely, between courses and actually while Benbow was eating. But nothing could spoil his appetite that night.

* * *

Gideon, on the other hand, felt sick to his heart and to his stomach.

He was in the candle-lit cellar of a house near the river, and it stank. Water had seeped in from the floor and the walls, and there was the stench of dampness and the odour of spices and stale meat, and the stench of urine and excrement. There were open privies and in holes dug in the ground, pits which no one had attempted to cover.

There were the women, and a few men.

There were the children, sleeping or drowsing.

There were the children-in-arms and at the breast: too often a dank and shrivelled, milkless breast.

And there were the rats; in the corners, creeping about the floors, tiny eyes like beads.

On the floor above, it was much the same; so it was next-door and next-door again and again and again.

On the top floors, conditions were slightly, very slightly better. There was electric light and gas to cook by, W.C.s which didn't work and closets which were stinking. There were bathrooms in which children slept and clothes hung to dry. In a corner, a policeman was quietly being sick.

Gideon looked at Piluski.

"Yes," he said. "We'll have the Press in, but we'll warn them what to expect first."

He was still nauseated when he got out into the street, where the air seemed to be contaminated, and answered questions from the waiting newspapermen, such as:

"Do you think this could be where typhoid starts, Commander?"

"Haven't the health and sanitary inspectors been here?"

"Did you find any signs of sabotage, Commander?"

When they had finished questioning him, they went in, and saw, and were silenced.

It was nearly nine o'clock when he arrived back at the Yard. Piluski was still at Battersea, but Rollo was in from Islington, and when Gideon looked into the control room he was leaning on his desk and saying to the men on night shift:

"I've never seen anything like it . . . Riddell only touched the surface . . . And if the Ministry of Health man is right, there's a child in one house with smallpox."
Rollo looked up, saw Gideon, and pushed his chair back. "That's true, sir," he went on doggedly. "It's a case of suspected smallpox."

"After what I've seen, I can believe it," Gideon said. "How many reports are in?"

Rollo glanced at a sergeant standing by a wall chart which hung from pins alongside the big maps. The round-faced, round-headed sergeant cast a perfunctory glance at the chart, and reported:

"Twenty-two so far, sir, and an additional eleven venues have been added to the original thirty. All venues have excessive overcrowding, but eleven have good to passable sanitary conditions. At least the plumbing works after a fashion. Some have communal kitchens and *crèches* and nurseries all provided by the landlords, but there are five very bad reports in addition to the one Mr. Rollo is telling us about, sir."

"Add the one where Mr. Piluski is, in Battersea," said Gideon. He beckoned Rollo who followed him out at once; the men in the room burst out as soon as they had gone:

"I thought Rollo looked bad enough, but Gee-Gee — "

"He looked as sick as a dog."

"My God, he looked awful."

"Tell you one thing," said the round-faced, round-headed sergeant, "there's going to be hell to pay for this." And when no one else made a comment, he went on: "I wonder how bad it would have got if

Gee-Gee hadn't started the raids. Been a new bloody plague of London, if you ask me."

CHAPTER 19

THE WITNESSES

"COLONEL SCOTT - MARLE, please," Gideon said into the telephone, a little later.

"That's Mr. Gideon, isn't it?" said Scott-Marle's wife. "I'll get him for you." She appeared to leave the instrument and there were voices in the background before she came on the line again. "What a lovely evening we had at the Ball," she went on. "I was sorry only that I wasn't able to spend more time with you and Mrs. Gideon."

Gideon thought almost fiercely: *Where's Scott-Marle?* He said: "Very nice of you, but there'll be another time. How are you?" *Where is Scott-Marle?*

"Very well, thank you — "

"George," Scott-Marle said obviously from the extension.

"I'll say good-bye," said his wife, as if sensing the urgency.

"Sir," said Gideon, "we have found at least five places which I think should be

290

examined by the Home Secretary himself, the Minister of Housing and the Minister of Health. There's no sign of sabotage as such, but conditions in these places are so appalling that they are undoubtedly a menace not only to the people who live in them but to public health."

Scott-Marle was silent for what seemed a long time; and then, with characteristic briskness and economy of words, he said:

"I will talk to the Home Secretary at once. When and where is it best to meet?"

"At Pentecost Street, Battersea," Gideon answered. "There will be patrols on duty along the various routes, sir. It's half-past nine now; I should think half-past ten will be a good time."

"I will do what I can. What about the Press, George?"

"They've been present and will stay in strength," Gideon answered. "I don't think either of the Ministers will be well-advised to stay away, sir."

"I see," Scott-Marle said. "I shall be there, in any case. Good-bye." He rang off without giving Gideon a chance to speak again.

Gideon, back in his own office, replaced

the telephone. He had expected nothing less than this reaction from Scott-Marle but was by no means certain that the politicians would respond. Much would depend on how Bartlett had presented his case, and how seriously the Cabinet really considered the over-all situation of immigration and racial conflict. There was the Enoch Powell school, trying to lessen the number here, and there were the left-wingers who wanted to open Britain wide to all immigrants. The awful truth was that these places they had discovered tonight were a result of illegal immigration. There couldn't be any doubt that if there was to be so much immigration, conditions must be right for it. His task was not to think one way or the other: simply to consider the consequences of such overcrowding.

Of course, it would be a health danger.

And of course there would be the habitual theft of money, anything saleable, and food, by the younger people who were on the point of starvation. There would be other thefts, of clothes, for instance, of anything for warmth.

His internal telephone bell rang; it didn't matter how late one was at the office, there was always someone with work for him to do.

"Gideon."

"Rollo here, sir."

"Be at Pentecost Street before ten-thirty," ordered Gideon. "And Piluski had better be there, too." After a pause he went on: "There should be a cloud of V.I.P. witnesses."

"There can't be too many," Rollo replied grimly. "But there is another development which could cause a lot of headaches, sir."

"What development?" demanded Gideon.

"The rent collector, Munshi, is dead," Rollo announced.

It was a very bad moment, one when Gideon's spirits touched bottom. The pictures which would appear in the morning's paper, even on tonight's late television, would affect a lot of the immigrant population, probably stirring them to fierce rage and a wild desire for revenge. Who could blame them? And with Munshi dead —

"What are the latest reports on the Munshi affair?" Gideon demanded.

"We've found two eye-witnesses, from houses nearby, who say that he fell down the steps and that two white youths began to kick him," stated Rollo. "We haven't caught the baskets yet, but one of them has been identified."

"Who's after him?" demanded Gideon.

"Chas Henry, at Hampstead; he's been seen by one of our chaps there."

"Is Superintendent Henry on duty to-night?" asked Gideon.

"Yes, sir."

"I'll talk to him," Gideon said. "And while you're on the line — "

"Sir?"

"Were any of the landlords we protected this morning involved in the places we've found tonight?"

"No, sir," answered Rollo. "At least, it's not yet established that any are. There *is* a kind of ring, though, with Rataudi and several others who permit their property to be used by illegal immigrants. Sub-letting has become a fine art."

"Are you *sure*?" Gideon almost barked.

"I'm sure the ring exists," Rollo affirmed. "I can't be absolutely sure that Rataudi is involved but it looks as if he is."

"Rollo," Gideon said tensely, "we need to know whether the bad — the worst — places seen tonight are all owned by the same landlords or the same ring. We need to find out if there are other landlords, outside this ring, who don't accept illegal immigrants and who keep their premises in reasonable condition."

"I *see*," said Rollo doubtfully, and then full understanding obviously dawned on him and he exclaimed: "If we can only tie up these plague spots with illegal entry, then we've got it high and dry as a criminal offence! My God! I'll put somebody on to that right away."

"Who've you got?" asked Gideon.

"Well — there's one man we could borrow from AB."

"Archer?"

"Yes."

"Get him," Gideon ordered. "Assign him to this part of the job. I'll have a word with Mr. Saxby." He rang off almost as abruptly as Scott-Marle had earlier, and immediately began to dial AB on his outside line. A Divisional operator answered.

"Mr. Saxby," Gideon said. "For Commander Gideon."

"One moment, sir." So Saxby was still working; everyone closely concerned with the collapse and immigration simply had to keep on, could not relax. After a few seconds, Saxby came on the line.

"What can I do for you, Commander?" There was the flatness of exhaustion in his voice.

"I would like Archer for a special job," Gideon said quietly.

"That'll please him," Saxby replied drily. "Do you want to see him yourself?"

"No. Send him over here to Rollo and Piluski, within the next half-hour if it's possible." Gideon paused, then added: "They know what the job is. Thanks." He rang off, and wiped some sweat off his forehead, realising to his surprise that he was feeling very hot. He sat back for a few minutes, then poured himself a whisky and soda with great care. For the first time since he had been to Pentecost Street he was actually hungry: after what he had seen he had felt that he would never eat again. He telephoned Henry at Hampstead to make sure he took charge personally of the search for the man who had kicked

Munshi, then pondered what to do for food.

He could have some sent here, or he could go up to the canteen.

He decided to go up; the office was not a good place to be at night, but before he went out he remembered Carol Entwhistle, and quite suddenly he realised that there was the Entwhistle case weighing on him, in its way as heavily as the other. He called *Information*.

"No, sir, no news," *Information* reported.

Gideon went upstairs, preferring to walk than use the lift. There were a dozen or so men in the canteen and the cafeteria was brightly lit. He went between the rails; simple food was probably best — ah! there was sausages and mash. He took a dishful, some rolls and butter and some coffee. Everyone in the place was looking at him, of course; that wasn't surprising. When he sat down to eat it was five minutes to ten. He ate steadily, going through the night's events in his mind, trying to make sure that he had forgotten nothing. He had telephoned Kate; he had checked about Riddell; he was up to date with all the other problems. Hobbs was now at Pentecost Street. How did such a fastidious man as Hobbs cope? Hobbs. It seemed ages ago but was only a few hours since he had decided that Hobbs should be the next Assistant Commissioner, not he!

How did he like that idea now that it had been in his mind for a while?

He speared a sausage, and said to himself: "I like the idea more and more." He heard footsteps nearby, someone looking for a table — but no, it was Honiwell, who did not have a tray in his hands. Honiwell's expression was very bright, he looked much better than when Gideon had last seen him, and Gideon's spirits rose.

"May I sit down, sir?"

"Yes. Have they found that child?"

"I only wish they had," Honiwell said, the brightness dimming. "It would be unbearable now if anything happened to her." He sat down, and Gideon was quite sure that he had good news. "We've found the evidence that Greenwood and Mrs. Entwhistle saw a lot of each other, sir. Absolutely cast iron."

Gideon's heart seemed to stop beating as he asked: "Can we prove it?"

"Beyond all doubt, sir. We can prove they were lovers, too."

Gideon buttered a piece of roll slowly and deliberately as he said: "Tell me," and then listened to Honiwell's version of Benbow's report. Benbow had discovered that there was a small guest house a few doors along from the restaurant, and the woman at the restaurant had told him that Greenwood occasionally stayed there. Benbow had gone to make inquiries, seen the register which went back several years, established the fact that rooms at the guest house were occasionally let by the hour or by the evening.

"And Greenwood and Margaret Entwhistle spent a lot of time in one of the private rooms," Honiwell said. "One old woman on the staff recognised both the photographs, and Greenwood signed the register. While this doesn't prove that Greenwood killed her it gives us a damned good reason for questioning him."

"When?" asked Gideon.

"Now," said Honiwell promptly.

"Let me know what happens," Gideon approved. "I'll be here or at home by midnight."

Honiwell went off with great eagerness, while Gideon followed him and went down in the lift this time, collected his coat from his office and went down the steps to the courtyard where a car was waiting. In fifteen minutes, at twenty-five past ten, he was outside the rat-infested hole where he had already been once tonight. There was a mob of people, dozens of newspapermen and a great flashing of camera-bulbs: so someone of importance was there! He stopped his car a little way ahead and went on by foot, so that no one was likely to be attracted by him.

There was Scott-Marle, Hobbs, the Rt. Honourable James Teddall, the Home Secretary, a pale-faced man whom Gideon recognised as Lord Windlesey, the stand-in for the Minister of Health, who was in Scotland. As they walked into the house and the cameras flashed and clicked, a man said:

"Well, they're taking it seriously this time."

Gideon was not recognised until he was at the entrance to one of the houses, and by then it was too late to be photographed or questioned, for obviously he had to hurry. He was behind the group of V.I.P.s as they went down to the cellar, saw the damp streaming from the walls and the rats not even frightened. The Home Secretary and Lord Windlesey were shocked into silence, so was the Minister of Housing, who arrived soon afterwards. Gideon waited until they had seen all they needed to see, and then joined the group. Hobbs, characteristically, drew out of range and earshot. Scott-Marle, brows knitted together and looking older than his years, was saying:

"It hardly seems to matter whose responsibility it is, Minister." That was to Windlesey. "What matters first is to cure it to prevent it from happening anywhere else, and to catch the men criminally responsible. I — " He broke off at the sight of Gideon, and seemed actually relieved. "Ah, Commander." There was a moment for introductions, before Scott-Marle asked:

"Have you any fresh information for us, Commander?"

"Yes," Gideon answered. "Most if not all of the people here were brought in illegally. The owners of the property almost certainly knew it, and gave them shelter. If you can call this shelter. They are jointly responsible for the immigrants. Even if they didn't actually help to smuggle them in they made it possible for them to stay, which is illegal harbouring. I think we may hope to bring criminal charges against some, if not all, of the landlords. Inquiries are being made throughout the night, and we might have some positive information tomorrow."

The Home Secretary said with vehemence: "It can't be soon enough, Commander."

"The main problem is to find somewhere for these people to live," Gideon said grimly.

"We are commandeering church and school halls," Lord Windlesey volunteered. "Places where they can be looked after and yet isolated for the time being. What I can't understand — " he gulped, and repeated: "What I can't understand is how people can make money out of creating such conditions, make money on the agony of other human beings. And their own countryfolk — "

Gideon said grimly: "I think we shall find that when it comes to money-making, there is no colour bar."

Soon, he was outside, and the night air was heavy with the odour from the houses, and yet comparatively fresh. The Home Secretary and the Ministers had gone, and Gideon stood with Scott-Marle and Hobbs at a corner near the row of houses. A few cameramen remained, but the three police leaders were not harassed.

"I'm tempted to say drop everything and concentrate on this." Scott-Marle said. "But you can't of course. I don't need to ask you to put every possible man on to it, do I?"

"No sir," Gideon said.

"Excuse me, sir," said a man who had come from a police car, "there's an urgent message for Mr. Gideon. *Information*'s on the radio now, sir."

It's from Honiwell, Gideon thought but said nothing as he hurried to the car, heart in mouth because of the possibility of hearing good news of Carol Entwhistle.

Instead, it was Wilson of EF Division, who spoke as he had always spoken in the past day or so, with elation in his voice. And because it was so obvious, it raised Gideon's spirits a little.

"We've got Rosamund Lee's murderer, sir! It was that Wells man. My bright young P.C. recognised him on his bicycle tonight, and he was caught trying to dump the bicycle in the Thames. Once he was stopped he didn't attempt to deny the charge. After a formal confession which we have signed and witnessed, sir, all he could talk about was his wife, poor bitch. She's got three kids, and ..."

Wilson went on and on.

*   *   *

Ellen Wells heard what the detective sergeant said, but could not really take it in. David, accused of murder. *David*. And she had to tell the children. She had to live alone. Oh God, she screamed within herself, I can't stand it, I can't stand it!

Percival Oswald, who did not know why he was so interested in this shabby, worn-out-looking woman, sensed her despair and wondered how he could help her. He went for the woman who lived upstairs, and brought her down — scared, troubled, excited, but at least willing to help.

Oswald had a peculiar thought: he almost wished he had not seen Ellen

Wells's husband, had not been so sure he was the murderer.

★   ★   ★

"George," Hobbs said, as they sat together in the back of a car and headed for Battersea Bridge, "let me drop you at home. I'll go on to the Yard to see if there's anything to be done. It's nearly midnight, and you look all in."

"Just check *Information* to find if there's any word from Honiwell," Gideon said. "I can't bear to think of that child."

CHAPTER 20

VISITORS

CAROL ENTWHISTLE stumbled along the path, hardly able to keep her balance, hardly able to think, going on with a kind of mechanical movement, perhaps sensing that if she collapsed she would probably never get up again. She was so cold, now, and it was terribly dark; she thought it was darker than it had been all night. She had no idea how long she had been walking, she only knew that she could not go on much longer.

Then, she heard a panting sound — in her ears, as if it were her own breathing.

A moment later she saw a vague circle of light, and a pale reflection on the mist. She tried to cry out but could not, tried to hurry but could not; and, trying to quicken her pace, she kicked against a stone and pitched forward.

The circle of light was from a torch held by a middle-aged policeman, who had known these moors since childhood and had taken part in dozens of hunts for escaped prisoners. Under his arm was a shotgun, by his side a young soldier strode with an Alsatian pulling at his leash. All over the moor there were such couples.

The policeman said: "This path crosses another, not far away, and we'll go on as far as that."

"I don't know how you can be sure you're where you think you are." The soldier looked at the mist which, even as close as this, made a halo about the policeman's profile. "I wouldn't have turned off the road."

"I know where I am," the policeman asserted confidently, "but I wouldn't like to step on to the moor. What's the matter with your dog?"

The soldier said: "He can smell a rabbit, I daresay." The dog was pulling very hard now, obviously aware of something ahead, and the policeman changed the beam of his torch trying to make it pierce further into the fog. All about them was silence, and nothing but mist was in sight.

The dog pulled harder.

"Careful," the policeman said, and he stopped and levelled the shotgun, then challenged: "Welbeck! Give yourself up."

There was no reply but the dog's panting. "Welbeck! You haven't a chance!"

"Do you really think it's him?" asked the soldier.

"I know it might be. Will you take the torch?" The policeman handed the torch over and then called again into the eerie gloom. "Welbeck! Give yourself up!"

The soldier shone the torch forward, at waist height; perhaps they could see for ten yards, straight ahead, at about the level a man's waist would be, but they could see neither above that level nor below. The dog was straining forward very hard now, there was no doubt at all that he had made some discovery.

The soldier said: "Can't you call for help?"

"I don't want to use the whistle unless I'm sure. *Welbeck!*" The policeman took a short step forward, straining to reach the centre of the haze of light, not even thinking of looking towards the ground.

He kicked against something.

"God!" he gasped, and staggered, then straightened up. The soldier shone the torch downwards and it shone on the path and gravel and a shoe: a child's shoe. The dog was pulling harder than ever, and panting louder, but above the sound of the panting was another sound: of crying.

Next moment the glow of the light fell about Carol Entwhistle as she half-stood, half-crouched, her eyes glistening in fear as the dog strained towards her. The next moment, at a word from the soldier, it was sitting and looking up at her, and the policeman was on one knee in front of her, putting an arm round her shoulders, soothing her, and saying: "There, there, it's all right. There, there."

★　★　★

Some two hundred miles away, in King's Road, Chelsea, where there was no more than a hint of fog, *Information* was saying to Gideon and Hobbs as they sat in the back of the car:

"Nothing yet from Mr. Honiwell, sir, but the child has been found. She was on the moor all right. Not hurt, according to the first reports."

"Thank God for that," Gideon breathed, and as he put the receiver down on a hook at the back of the driver's seat, he went on: "All right, Alec. I'll go home."

As they headed towards Fulham and Harrington Street, only ten minutes drive away, the radio was filled with the happenings of the night: of calls for help, reports of burglaries, reports of accidents; they reached *Information* in a never-ending stream, as the war against crime was waged unceasingly through most of London's night.

* * *

But Eric Greenwood was not asleep, he was wide awake. He had been reading and listening to a late night orchestral concert on B.B.C.3, his head filled with vague thoughts of Jennifer, of what he would have to do, of his coming "holiday", of the fact that the *Orianda* was making good progress and would be here a day early unless she ran into trouble in the Bay of Biscay, when there had been a ring at his flat bell. Instantly he had thought: Jennifer. He put down the book, a biography of one of the early members of the East India Company, out of which Cox and Shieling had been born, and went to the door, anger beginning to rise.

Two big men, undoubtedly policemen,

stood at the door. The bigger of the two, wearing a huge overcoat, was a stranger. The other man was familiar — a bruiser type with broken nose and flattened lips; he had seen him about the office area, in the pub where he and Bessie went occasionally.

The bigger man spoke.

"Mr. Eric Greenwood?"

"I — yes. Yes."

"My name is Honiwell, Chief Superintendent Honiwell of New Scotland Yard," the speaker announced. From the depths of his clothes he took a card and handed it to Greenwood. "This is Detective Sergeant Benbow."

"What — what can I do for you?" Greenwood made himself ask. He stood blocking the doorway, so shocked that it didn't occur to him to ask them in. He had no idea why they had come, did not give a thought to the murder he had committed four years ago.

"May we come in, sir?" asked Honiwell.

"I — er — I was just going to bed. I — yes, come in." He led them into the pleasant room where the strains of the B.B.C. orchestra sounded gentle and soothing. "What — er — is everything all right?" Suddenly it dawned on him that there must have been a burglary at the warehouse or the showrooms: why else should the police have sent senior officers? "What's happened?" he demanded.

"Mr. Greenwood," Honiwell said in a heavy, doom-laden voice, "we wish to know why, when we were asking in the newspapers for information about a Mrs. Margaret Entwhistle after she had been murdered, you did not come forward with information." Honiwell turned to Benbow. "What was the name of that restaurant in Fulham Road?"

"The English Fayre," Benbow answered flatly.

"And the guest house where Mr. Greenwood and Mrs. Entwhistle stayed from time to time?"

"Evergreens."

Greenwood was staring as if he could not believe this was happening. He had gone chalk-white. His hands clenched by his side and his breath whistled through his nostrils.

"Now, sir. Your explanation, please," Honiwell growled. He looked so big and menacing, and Benbow had a savage expression. He moved to one side, doubled his right fist and raised his arm up and down.

"I — I — I — " stammered Greenwood.

Honiwell dived with his right hand into his coat, the swift movement making Greenwood sway backwards. He brought out two photographs, the top one of Margaret Entwhistle as she had lain on the morgue slab, the other of her laughing with her children. Honiwell held them like two cards in a pack and thrust them in front of the frightened man.

"Perhaps this will help you remember," he growled.

Greenwood was now swaying on his feet, and slowly turning green. Suddenly he backed away and dropped into his chair, trembling violently. Honiwell and Benbow exchanged a quick, satisfied glance, as Honiwell dropped the morgue photograph on to Greenwood's knees.

* * *

Gideon was getting into bed when the telephone bell rang, and Kate was lying on her side, looking at him. He slid into bed before picking up the telephone. There was light from street lamps as well as from the bedside table, and in the glow of this, the pyjama'd Gideon looked enormous. Certainly no one would call him at this hour unless it were urgent.

"Gideon," he said.

"We've got Greenwood," Honiwell announced with a lilt in his voice. "We've a confession, signed, irretractable, I would say. He killed her because she wanted to tell her husband and get a divorce and he didn't want to marry and thought a divorce would upset his employers. They're a pretty puritanical lot, as far as I can see." Honiwell was talking a little too much but no one had earned the right to talk more. "We've got him at the Yard, sir."

"Good!" Gideon enthused. "I couldn't be more glad. Now you'll have some news to take to Dartmoor tomorrow." He would have rung off then, but sensed that Honiwell still had something to say, and asked: "What else, Matt?"

"I bumped into Piluski at the Yard," said Honiwell, "and went into that Operations Room. They're making quite a job, sir!" Hastily Honiwell went on: "But the point is, among the landlords on their list there's Cox and Shieling, Limited. The same company has a line of cargo vessels which run from the Far East via Bombay, and Karachi — Pakistan and some other port. I just wondered if they traffic in illegal immigrants. Just an idea, sir."

"We'll find out first thing in the morning," Gideon said grimly.

Tired as he was, he did not get to sleep quickly. The strange thing was that he was most preoccupied with the thought of Entwhistle and his years under a life sentence as well as with the young Church of England priest who had first persuaded him, Gideon, to look into the case, despite the fact that it had been officially over and done with for years.

* * *

On the following day, in the middle of the afternoon, Honiwell arrived at Dartmoor Prison; he had travelled by early train to Exeter and been met by a police car at the station. He had visited the policeman's cottage where Carol was still sleeping, cared for by the policeman's wife, and was now taken to the Governor, who reminded him startlingly of a younger Scott-Marle.

"Well, Superintendent," the Governor said, "I'm very glad we found the child. We wouldn't have if the prisoner Welbeck hadn't escaped, because we wouldn't have had a search party out."

"Have you found Welbeck yet, sir?"

"No. We keep getting rumours that he's been seen. Got away on a motor-cycle, apparently." The Governor shrugged that off, and went on: "Commander Gideon tells me you have some remarkably good news for the prisoner Entwhistle."

"*Very* good news, sir," Honiwell said.

"And I understand that the Home Secretary has ordered his transfer from Dartmoor to Brixton, where he will stay until the formalities are concluded. Of course the transfer will be arranged at once." He pressed a bell, and almost immediately the door opened and the chief warder appeared. "Fetch Entwhistle will you?" said the Governor. "Just tell him that I want to see him."

* * *

Entwhistle was in the one place where he could get some peace of mind: the library.

He was alone, for most of the prisoners were confined to their cells; there was always tension in the air during an escape, always danger that hotheads would start trouble. Entwhistle was surprised he had been allowed to come to the library. When the chief warder came for him in person he assumed it was to do with Welbeck's escape, and even when he was told that he was going to see the Governor, he thought the same thing. He would have leapt to the wildest conclusions at any other time.

There was the Governor, behind his desk, a big man whom Entwhistle didn't know, and the chief warder, on the other side of the desk. It was at this moment that he realised this was not simply about Welbeck.

"Entwhistle," the Governor said, "this is Chief Detective Superintendent Honiwell, of New Scotland Yard. He has been making inquiries over several months into the circumstances surrounding the murder of your wife, and he has good news for you."

Entwhistle felt as if every nerve in his body, every muscle too, had gone as stiff as steel. Only two words went through his

317

mind, over and over again. *Good news, good news, good news*. The chief warder drew closer to him, for he looked as if he were about to faint, and Honiwell came towards him, hand outstretched.

"We now know that another man killed her," Honiwell said as he shook hands in an almost casual way. "And we have the man under arrest. There will be a number of formalities, Mr. Entwhistle, but I have Home office permission to assure you that there will be a minimum of delay until your release."

Entwhistle said in a husky voice: "Release. Release." He felt the chief warder guiding him to a chair. "*Release.*" His mind was in hopeless confusion, there was now a medley of words. "Good news — another man killed her — release. *Release.*" He felt his nerves relaxing. He felt a whisky flask pressed to his lips. "My God!" he gasped. "I'm cleared!" Now, his eyes blazed. "I'm cleared." And then he got up slowly and turned to the Governor. "When — when can I see my children, sir?" But he wasn't thinking of all three children, he was thinking of Carol.

Very gently, the Governor told him

what Carol had done and where she was; and a radiance began to grow in Entwhistle's gaunt face. Radiance.

CHAPTER 21

LONG AND SHORT TERM

"I DON'T mind admitting I wasn't far from tears myself," Honiwell said to Gideon, two days later. He had just come back with Entwhistle and the child. Entwhistle was now in a remand cell at Brixton, with privileges he had not had in years, and Carol was at home with her aunt. The story of her journey and the story of Greenwood's arrest had hit the headlines this morning, the first sensation to drive off the pictures and stories of the immigrants' plight. "They just stared at each other, sir. They just stared. And it was Entwhistle who broke down. He began to cry. And he went down on his knees to her." Honiwell gulped. "If I live to be a hundred. I'll never see anything like that again."

Gideon said quietly: "I hope you never have to, Matt. You and Benbow did a remarkable job. Remarkable." He waited for a few moments and then went on: "Well, you'll have plenty to do getting this case cleared up, but when you're not on it, give Rollo and Piluski a hand, will you? You'll be interested to know that the partners in Cox and Shieling Limited as well as the Company itself are owners of a great deal of property tenanted by Pakistani immigrants, and all their property is maintained, with good order under strict supervision. Three out of four such places we've seen are, thank God. But there are far too many bad ones and Rataudi is part owner of most of these. He has an English and a Jamaican and a Chinese partner."

"It's going to take a hell of a long time to get to the bottom of that job," Honiwell said.

"Yes," Gideon agreed. "A very long time. But we've now done so much and the Government has taken it so seriously that everyone concerned is satisfied that the authorities are trying to make sure that all parties get justice. That should really be enough to calm things down."

* * *

It was going to take months and possibly years to sort out the criminal from the civil offences where the immigrants' housing was concerned, as well as the different forms of illegal entry, Gideon knew. But there were clear indications that emergency housing arrangements were being made at speed. There were other goods things, too: the discovery at Pentecost Street as well as the disaster at Long Street had shocked most people, particularly many of the anti-coloured population. There were calls for stricter control of immigration, there was need to put more police on to the investigation of smuggling at airports and seaports. There were calls for a census of non-white population, for a thorough check throughout the land of the conditions in which they worked and lived.

But the duty of the police was now well-defined.

It looked to Gideon as if Rollo and Piluski, as well as Archer and later, Honi-well, would be assigned to all the police aspects of the situation for a long time to come. There might be a case for setting up a department in the Home Office, C.I.D., and provincial forces, as well as customs, Port of London Authority, airport and dock-side police forces, but the time wasn't yet.

There were other, long-term problems.

Of the new Assistant Commissioner, for instance. He had persuaded Scott-Marle to continue as they were for a few months, and he knew exactly what he was going to do: have Hobbs stand in for him with increasing frequency so that Scott-Marle not only got to know the other more as a man, but came to understand Hobbs's qualities.

There was the preparation of the papers for the trial of David Wells; the quicker they went to the Public Prosecutor's office, the better.

There was the search for the missing antique dealer, Max, who had not been found, despite a squeal.

There was the trial of the two men who had been caught burgling Max's shop.

There was formal approval to be given, once the insurance companies had been over all the recovered stolen property, for its return to the owners. There would be a lot of satisfaction over that, and he wondered whether one of the national newspapers could be persuaded to feature the story: it was time attention was focused on the good side of police work instead of on the sensational and the sordid.

And there was the dealing, day by day, with the crime of London, including the big embezzlement case.

As he stood at his window, after Honiwell had gone, he wondered again what new crimes were being planned, what new horror and what new dread; what grief and dismay was waiting, all unsuspected, for the ordinary people. And he thought too, of those who were in such trouble now and of those who narrowly escaped it.

* * *

Jennifer Goodenough was at the quayside when the *Orianda* docked, and was among the first to go aboard. She seemed to be followed by a shadow, of what might have been had Eric not been arrested and charged. As she went towards the bridge where she would find Simon, she touched her throat and mouth with her hands.

Ellen Wells was in a curiously unreal frame of mind; doing everything she had to do for the children, seeing Welfare and other authorities because her income had been cut off, and aware of the kindness and compassion of so many people, including the police. In a strange way, it was a relief. She had always dreaded what would happen if David left her, and now she knew. The chief concern was for the children. She might have to move away from here, but whatever happened, she now knew that she could cope.

So did Violet Riddell.

Her Tom was coming home in a day or two, but he would need a great deal of looking after, would be convalescent for weeks, perhaps for months. The wonderful thing was that he had been asked whether he would like to go to one of the police nursing and convalescent homes, or come home to her. And he had chosen to come home. She would have something worthwhile to do at last; look after him, nurse him, do anything he needed. She could mother him! They had never had a child, and she wouldn't know herself.

And she would never forget that he *wanted* to come home.

There was another thing she mustn't forget, either; he was a hero. Why, there was already talk that he should be recommended for the George Medal, the most important civil award for bravery.

Violet Riddell had never been so happy in her married life.

And Netta Jameson, who now called herself Honiwell, had never been so deeply contented. She was even thinking of giving up the *salon* so as to be at home whenever Matthew had a few hours off. She wasn't quite sure whether this would be wise, but before long she would have a word with Kate Gideon about it. No one was likely to know more about the needs of a policeman.

MYSTERY TITLES IN THE ULVERSCROFT LARGE PRINT SERIES

OCTAVO SIZE

Police at the Funeral	*Margery Allingham*
Death of a Ghost	*Margery Allingham*
A Kind of Anger	*Eric Ambler*
The Night They Killed Joss Varran	
	George Bellairs
The Sad Variety	*Nicholas Blake*
The Thirty-Nine Steps	*John Buchan*
In Spite of Thunder	*J. Dickson Carr*
The Saint on Guard	*Leslie Charteris*
The Saint Around the World	
	Leslie Charteris
The Mirror Crack'd from Side to Side	
	Agatha Christie
Ordeal by Innocence	*Agatha Christie*
Cards on the Table	*Agatha Christie*
Death on the Nile	*Agatha Christie*
Endless Night	*Agatha Christie*
Towards Zero	*Agatha Christie*
The Murder of Roger Ackroyd	
	Agatha Christie
Dumb Witness	*Agatha Christie*
Murder in Mesopotamia	*Agatha Christie*

The Clocks	*Agatha Christie*
The Moving Finger	*Agatha Christie*
Sad Cypress	*Agatha Christie*
The Mists of Fear	*John Creasey*
A Gun for Inspector West	*John Creasey*
Send Superintendent West	*John Creasey*
Nothing is the Number When You Die	
	Joan Fleming
The Long Short Cut	*Andrew Garve*
The Laughing Grave	*Victor Gunn*
The Next One to Die	*Victor Gunn*
The Unfinished Clue	*Georgette Heyer*
Death on Doomsday	*Elizabeth Lemarchand*
Gideon's Day	*J. J. Marric*
Gideon's Week	*J. J. Marric*
The Eye of a Serpent	*Geoffrey Peters*
The Dog Man	*Maurice Procter*
Devil's Due	*Maurice Procter*
If Death Ever Slept	*Rex Stout*
The Mystery of Swordfish Reef	
	Arthur Upfield

This book is published under the auspices of the ULVERSCROFT FOUNDATION, a registered charity, whose primary object is to assist those who experience difficulty in reading print of normal size.

In response to approaches from the medical world, the Foundation is also helping to purchase the latest, most sophisticated medical equipment desperately needed by major eye hospitals for the diagnosis and treatment of eye diseases.

If you would like to know more about the ULVERSCROFT FOUNDATION, and how you can help to further its work, please write for details to:

THE ULVERSCROFT FOUNDATION
Station Road
Glenfield
Leicestershire

We hope this Large Print edition gives you the pleasure and enjoyment we ourselves experienced in its publication.

There are now over 700 titles available in this ULVERSCROFT Large Print Series. Ask to see a Selection at your nearest library.

The Publisher will be delighted to send you, free of charge, upon request a complete and up-to-date list of all titles available.

Ulverscroft Large Print Books Ltd.,
Station Road, Glenfield,
Leicester, England.